Time Walker Chronicles:
Volume 1

Filling the Void

P.D. Kew

Email: pd.kew.writer@gmail.com

Author's First Edition

ISBN 978-0-9854334-2-0

For Mitsy

Chapter 1

Yellow ochre sky in morning,
Time Walker take warning.

                                --Anon

"You really fucked this one, Mitch," Aunt Jenny had said yesterday at John's funeral. "This was on *your* watch."

Her words still burned in my ears as I swirled the dregs in the bottom of my coffee cup. I needed a real drink.

John.

I had driven most of the night and had stopped for a bite to eat at a roadside diner on the outskirts of Moscow, Idaho. A threadbare velvet rope hung across the entrance to the darkened bar.

Out the wide window next to me, I gazed across the dirty ice-crusted vacant parking lot. Past my pickup, the snow-capped hills of the Palouse Range to the north stretched from horizon to horizon.

The morning sky was indeed ochre as a
Rising winter sun began its daily climb out
of the east to its death in the west.

Yes, I was once a poet. Not a good one as is evident from my verse: too many metaphors in the mix, and my symbolism

5

has always sucked. 'Am I the sun?' The usual shit. But, I had had some of my scrawls published even though I was never any good at French. Helps to flash in as a woman in cases such as this. You could get a bit more mileage with artistic things.

"More coffee, honey?" the waitress asked.

I pushed my cup toward her. "What time does the bar open?"

She cringed. "It's a bit early—"

"I'm well aware of the time. Believe me. Gin would be good if you can manage one. Straight. No ice."

With the bottom of my right fist, I banged the GPS. The device glowed on the table in front of me, the display still stuck in Bombay as it continued to "re-calculate" or whatever the fuck it was doing. It'd given out south of McCall. I held a patent for the damn technology, too, but I never used these things. Ever since I'd crewed on the *Victoria*, it seemed kind of pointless. Didn't really matter anyway. I was on the doorstep of the Palouse Range. I'd be deep in those welcoming mountains by this time tomorrow.

The crowd was pretty thin, as one would expect on a Monday morning. A few fat truckers trying for the lone waitress, "Eloise" her name tag read, a woman in her late thirties who had the look of being ridden too hard and put away wet.

There's something about bars and alcohol. Temporarily blinds the trenchies. Has to do with the Theory of Manifold Arrangement and Hodge's Law. But, I'm not Tech, so I'm not good with the "how." To me, it's just another tool in the Time Walker arsenal.

"Happy to see me, Mitch?" z said.

I leaned back in the red linoleum booth, and with my foot I tried to drag the token bag toward me. z stood at the edge of the table, staring down at me as only z could.

"Look who the fucking Cheshire Cat drug in," I said. "You're coming way late in my cycle, z."

"Yeah," z idly scratched. "About that. Your cycle. Your brief."

"Fuck."

z plopped down into the booth opposite me and looked around the bar. "Nice place you've discovered. The Wagon Wheel Bar and Grill! I simply love the urbane cowboy décor. In Moscow, Idaho no less! The *Esto Perpetua* state. Appropriate for us, yes?"

I pointed to the ceiling. "Hear that? They're playing *Queen*. Your favorite. Can't be all that bad if—"

z held a hand up.

I stopped.

"We'll always have Moscow, right?" z winked. "Of course I'm right. Now. On to business. Struggling a bit with this brief of yours, are we?"

I sat up in the booth, the friction of my body making farting sounds on the linoleum. "Shit. I'm not out-synched again, am I?"

"No," z said. "No, not out-synched. If only it was as easy as that. They have a decent whiskey here?"

As z tried to get Eloise's attention, I hooked the token bag with my boot toe.

"Excuse me!" z said to the waitress, who was finally within earshot. "Madam. Yes. Please..."

I pulled the bag closer to me. Inch by inch, centimeter by centimeter.

"I need a whiskey," z said to Eloise.

Something rattled out of the bag onto the wood floor underneath the table.

"Yes, Jack will do," z said. "It's not whiskey or even whisky. But, it will do. I have the original recipe for it, by the way..."

Fuck!

"Why, yes, I'm foreign!" z said. "Good girl! You picked up on my accent. Are you a government agent hiding out here?"

I'd inadvertently scattered the contents of the bag underneath the table. I tried to gather the tokens with my feet.

"Do I look like a terrorist to you?" z laughed, taking the bourbon-filled tumbler from Eloise. "I normally reserve acts of terrorism for bed. Now go, young lady."

z turned back to me. "Your brief, Mitch. We're on the cusp. Right now."

"John was hit by them," I said, "We're not responsible for the indirects. You know that better than I do."

z's eyebrows raised. "Indirects are..."

Another rattle from under the table. I stilled my foot. I lost track of what z was saying.

"...matter at all," z said. "Particularly since you jump in two days."

* * *

It all started with John's death.

No one understands, though. The bullet was meant for me.

They think I'm all cut up about John's death because...well, let them think it. It was entirely platonic. I knew Plato when he was a lad, and you'd have a different idea of what "platonic" meant if you knew what Plato did as a lad. But I mean it as you understand it.

I had gone with John to that kind of neighborhood because he believed in self-medication, and it was the only way he could ease the pain of his esophageal cancer. He didn't talk much. He never had. That's why I liked to be with him.

Everyone thinks it was a drive-by. A gangland killing.

We had just left the house in the Boise suburbs. A troop of girl scouts selling cookies door-to-door stood between the car and us. John wanted to avoid them, so we walked once around the cul-de-sac. When we were opposite the car, the Mercedes sped into the cul-de-sac and skidded in a loop. Everyone froze and watched as the Mercedes narrowly missed the girl scouts.

I noticed the yellow ochre trench coat. The arm extended from the passenger window with a revolver at the end of the yellow ochre sleeve.

They always come in yellow ochre. And they'll come again. And again.

Once in Rome he had come in a yellow ochre toga. It seems someone else always gets it first as a warning. Why they warn me, I'll never know. The blade at the end of the yellow toga's sleeve plunged into the neck and chest for wounds number twenty and twenty-one. The total was supposed to be twenty-four, but I just couldn't do my part. The first five had sufficed for their immediate purpose. The rest were for symbolism and bragging rights. Within three days, I had moved on.

Now I have two days to get to that meadow in the mountains.

John got the bullet. It wasn't meant for me in the sense that they had tried to kill me. It was meant for me as the warning that my time was coming. Time to move on. Just as with Caesar. Just as with Trotsky. And just as with Willy Loman. Just as with countless others, famous, infamous, and ignorous.

I just have to stay a step ahead of them for two days. Next time the bullet will be for me. That's why after the funeral I had my pickup serviced. I didn't want any mishaps on my way to the mountains.

The most fundamental law of the infiniteverse is this: shit happens. It's always been true and always will be. You can't keep mundane circumstances from complicating your ambitions. But you can mitigate the effects of such complications by being vigilant and taking pains with the details that are within your control. That is the second-most fundamental law of the infiniteverse: give it your best effort and you'll end up okay. I should know. I've been around.

The waiting room of the auto shop reminded me of the waiting room at the hospital where we waited for word on John's operation. The doctor came out and just shook his head. I waited for the mechanic to do the same.

"Sorry, I did all I could, but the fuel injector has pneumonia and the block is cracked. It's only a matter of time. You can say your goodbyes."

That's what the funeral had for me. Not just goodbye to John, but to everyone. You never get used to saying goodbye. You make a lot of close friends in twenty-five years. Now I say goodbye and in two days I become twenty-years-old again somewhere else. No idea what my purpose is. Just get along the best I can. Somewhere along the way, I'll inadvertently do what they send me there to do. They say it's better I don't know my brief. They don't want me trying too hard.

"You're good to go," the mechanic said.

Good to go. If he only knew the full extent of those words.

The pickup was prepared. After tying up a few more details, I was off to the mountains.

I've seen the location on the satellite map. I have the coordinates in my GPS. A few times I've missed the first opportunity to flash, but only once did I miss the second. She was a chief rabbi's wife in seventeenth-century Amsterdam, and I was ready to give it all up for her. I had fully accepted mortality and was ready to ignore the third and last opportunity to jump until I found her yellow ochre dress in the suitcase under the bed.

I bought a good coat. A warm outdoor coat. I'll have to leave the campsite in the morning and spend those next few hours in the snow hiking to the flash point. I don't like the cold.

Yellow ochre. I only know the ones who work against me by their yellow ochre clothing. That's another reason they don't tell me my brief. If I knew my brief, then my behavior would expose me to the trenchies as a Time Walker. As it is, they only get the scent of my trail when my time to flash draws near.

Those who direct my work aren't perfect, though. Sometimes they double-book an entry flash and the Time Walker spends twenty-five years as a schizophrenic. All the while, another being elsewhere spends that same quarter-century asleep, bereft of sentience. Rumor has it that was what happened to Rip van Winkle. They exit-flashed the twenty-to-forty-five year old Rip out to Khartoum, but on his entry flash, they waylaid the forty-five-to-seventy year old Rip in Bermuda. Took them twenty years to rectify the situation. They claimed the Time Walker missed his third flash on purpose to live out his life on the Bermuda beaches with the native women instead of with the healthy Dutch women in the land of Knickerbockers. I don't believe it at all.

Sometimes they mess up by getting our shifts out of phase. Once I flashed into two different humans. Both beings ended up half-wits. One was a bootlegger in the mountains of Appalachia, and the other the youngest son of a Boston socialite. I killed myself in the Battle of Appomattox. That is to say, the bootlegger killed the son of the socialite--in hand-to-hand combat no less. I remember the event from both perspectives. The look of fear and bloodlust reverberated through time like an infinite corridor of magic mirrors. They got me back on phase after that. The doctors would have called it a case of fugue. I would know. I was a doctor once. I also caught dengue fever while building the Panama Canal. The conditions are not related. The only similarity is the odd spelling ending in "-gue." I've been a grammarian too.

I work the twenty-to-forty-five shift. I like it. Height of a man's powers. Every twenty-five years you get the privilege of returning to the sins of your youth, but with more knowledge about how to make the most of it.

And now if I can just outrun those yellow ochre trench coats for two more days, I'll get that twenty-year old body once more. I could sure use one about now. I just hope they don't entry flash me as a woman like they did one time into Czarist Russia.

* * *

At John's funeral service at the church in Boise, Aunt Jenny and I stood toe-to-toe in the narrow pew. The infamous Aunt Jenny. Keeper of the purer faith and all of that bullshit.

All the while, John's casket loomed at the altar some twenty feet in front of us.

Michael approached us. Aunt Jenny flashed him a look then returned her stare to me.

"John wasn't supposed to die," she hissed at me. "I hope it was worth it. Do yourself a favor. Remember what I said. You'll see them soon enough."

"I always hate this part of a funeral," Michael said.

I stared at Aunt Jenny. "I know what you mean."

She left us and made her way toward the center aisle.

I sat next to Michael. Out over the pews were a dozen or so odd souls who'd come to this house of worship to bid John farewell. I recognized most of them. Business associates. Guys from his bowling team. Even his dealer. They all looked out of sorts, like something was missing, but they couldn't put their humble little minds on exactly what was causing their discomfort. John's early death? Who the hell knew.

I needed a drink.

"I went to a funeral once," Michael said.

"Just once?"

He ignored my remark. "I was at the...what would you call it...the reception?"

I looked at the altar. "The after-party."

The minister stepped up to the altar and opened his Bible.

Michael gritted his teeth and continued. "They just set up a microphone next to the cake and punch for those who wanted to say a few words. It's too intimidating to talk in an auditorium like this."

Aunt Jenny glanced at me over her shoulder from her seat a few pews in front.

"Crazy bitch," I muttered.

"Shut up, Mitch," Michael glared at me. "We're in a church, for Christ's sake!"

"Ah, yes," I said. "A church. Been a while. For a lot of things."

Michael was wistful. "It's like when the three of us used to—"

The minister cleared his throat. "I know a few of you would like to say a few words about John's life and his love for his family and his God."

Across this throng of John's "friends," a few people chose this time to clear their throats and noses. The pews creaked. The timid ones looked over their shoulders, hoping for someone to speak, dreading the thought that they'd be forced to speak.

"Well," said the minister. "I'll start by saying that John's love for God was important..."

Michael bumped me with his arm. He pointed at her. "Aunt Jenny is getting up to speak. That's classic! The minister isn't even done with his droning."

"I told you she's a crazy bitch."

"That's not nice," he said. "John meant a lot to her."

And what of me?

The hall, and finally the minister, fell silent at the approach of *the* Aunt Jenny, that wizened old windbag clicking up the aisle. The syncopated rhythm of her heels and cane set more than a few toes tapping.

"Thanks, Reverend," she said. "Johnny was a good boy. He always helped me out with my fantasy football picks. Good kid."

Fuck! She's pouring it on!

Aunt Jenny continued. "Now let's get out of this dreariness and get something to eat—for John."

Aunt Jenny clicked down the aisle and tugged on coat sleeves, urging people to follow her to the church's recreation room. Passing by my pew, she glared at me. I gave her the finger. I took care so only she could see it—and she did.

I winked at Michael. "I'm starved. Let's hope the bar is open."

Michael sprung up and offered his arm to Aunt Jenny. I headed toward the exit, making no attempt to gather people for the procession.

I did steal a glance back at the minister and saw his reaction at losing total control to that bitch Aunt Jenny.

"Join the club, bud," I said.

* * *

At the after-party, I thought about the jump.

Be yourself.

I'd jumped so many times. Had it down to a ritual. But, it wasn't perfect. Shit did happen.

"Where's your head, Mitch?" said Michael's mom.

I laughed. "Ask Michael!"

"He's going camping, mom," Michael said.

She raised her eyebrows. "You know it's December, right?"

"He's going to center himself," Michael said. "What with John's death and all."

"Just trying to be myself," I said, pounding back another glass of pinot noir. "Damn this is good stuff. Yes, I've packed all the standard equipment for a long weekend of camping. By myself."

I had just enough gas in the pickup to get close to the camping site before the jump. The best part of all this shit was when I stopped paying the bills and ran my credit cards up to the hilt.

I still had a girlfriend, too, even after I'd received the first sign that this day was coming. The past few months I'd held many dinner parties for friends and tried to create as many loose ends at work as possible.

Michael's mom said she wanted more cake, but when she saw the reverend setting up a microphone next to the cake table, she went for the wine bar instead.

"You off?" Michael asked.

"Yeah," I said.

"I'll walk you out"

We left the after-party and entered the Nave of the church.

"Have a safe trip," he said. "You're still on for bowling Tuesday, right?"

"Absolutely. I'll fill in for John. You can count on me."

Michael smiled. "Drive safe, Mitch."

I pushed him back. "We're in church for Christ's sake."

* * *

Back at the diner, z took another draw of bourbon. "This place is a wasteland," he said.

He paused as Eloise refreshed our water. "Anything else, gents?" she said.

z smiled. "You've done more than enough."

"Check, please," I said.

My eyes followed her all the way into the kitchen.

"Back to business, Mitch," z said. "Your jump. It's imperative you make this one. And I mean your first flash point."

I hated the jump.

Not so much the tingling of the field as you jumped, but the concept of what the flash point did. Didn't help when you heard the stories of a jump gone really bad. But, as I'd said, I'm not Tech. I have no idea how the machine works or the *Deus* within. Not my job. Not my concern.

"It's ironic," z said between swigs of bourbon. "You're scheduled to flash on the Winter Solstice!" z laughed. Hard. "With your history and all! A Solstice flash is —"

"Let's not get personal," I said. "There's a shit load of water that's gone under that particular bridge."

"Ironic to a tee," z said. "You always have been."

"What the hell do you want?" I asked.

z slammed the glass tumbler down on the wooden table. "You touched the Void last time you jumped. You know it's prohibited. It's a violation of standard protocol."

"That's it? That's why you're here?" I asked. "You're such an asshole when it comes to the rules and shit like that."

"You know the Logic and Rational Regression Sardonicies! You got the training. You don't get three outs this time!"

"What?" I asked.

z inhaled deeply, more out of irritation than anything else. "Listen, Mitch. You've got to make your primary flash point. Okay? No suckies or turid exit points. Get me?"

"Punishment?"

"You've got one door out of here," z said.

"Why?" I asked.

"Why?" z said. "Now that is the question."

A beat. Both of us looked out the window. A semi drove by on U.S. 95. The yellow ochre of the driver's shirt was barely visible as the rig turned north, heading for the wide expanse of the Palouse Range.

"Time for me to go," *z* said.

z emptied the glass in a single gulp and stood up.

"A word of advice, dear friend," *z* said. "If you make this jump, don't pick up the mirror on the other side. You won't like what you find staring back at you. *Adieu.*"

Chapter 2

Damn token bag. Damn *z*. The token bag is supposed to be discretely camouflaged against my side until I need it. Everything with it goes haywire when *z* shows up. *z*. Fuck *z*.

I untangled my feet from the cords of the bag. The tokens were still scattered on the floor under the bar. Can't believe a kid looks for a chance to climb under the table. The greasy, chewing-gum-coated bottom of a tabletop.

"Dad, I gotta pee," the kid shouted down the way.

"Go pee," dad said.

"Let me out!"

"Climb under the table."

"Can I really?"

I almost asked the kid if he'd pick up my things from the floor for a few bucks. But then I thought about what that would look like. Things like that don't go over well in places like Moscow, Idaho. Ancient Greece, maybe, but even then you have to be careful. Make sure it's Athens, not Sparta.

Tokens. Mementos of my previous incarnations. Sometimes tools, sometimes weapons, sometimes currency—both negotiable and non-negotiable—and sometimes just shit that I liked to keep to remember people and places. Random five-and-ten store flotsam. Rarely the jetsam. It's hard to keep such detritus in pairs.

Thanks to *z*, the figurative history of my life as a Time Walker was spread out on the floor, and I bent over to pick it all up. One-by-one. But something was missing.

I checked the contents several times, and could not place the missing piece. Too many items. The bag could hold much more than its external, visible volume suggested.

I scanned the floor. Checked the bottom of my feet.

Maybe z took it.

I'd lost things here and there, as most people do. Crossing dimensions and vast quantities of time and space was nothing compared to the daily entropy of mundane existence while living out an incarnation.

Something else had bit the dust, as Freddy says. But even knowing how way leads on to way, I sometimes find that the missing token appears once more in the unlikeliest of places. Maybe it's *z* playing games with me, as *z* is so fond of doing.

Still bent over, I tied the cords around the mouth of the bag and heard the annoying sound of liquid slurping into a coffee cup. Yeah, I could use the re-fill, but quieter, please. There's a flow, a measured flow at which the sound of liquid pouring into liquid isn't so full of discordant overtones.

It's not Eloise.

I stood up. It wasn't Eloise. But why I had this thought or made this distinction was beyond me. What the hell did I care about Eloise?

Glenda was older, fatter, ridden harder, and wetter than Eloise. (Wetter in a non-sexual, non-metaphorical way.)

"She's on her smoke break," the black-haired too-many-pounds-of-flesh said as she dribbled a little more coffee into my cup.

I must have reacted to the noise of the coffee.

"Why all you scoundrels are after that skank, I'll never understand," Glenda said. "Men," she said in a huff.

"Splash of vodka if you don't mind, sexy?" I said. Never hurt to try to butter any woman up a little, even those you would never touch with your ten-foot...you know.

"Eloise told me to watch out for you. Fucking lush. Ain't your mama teach you how to live a right and upstanding life?"

"I don't remember my mama," I said, maybe a little too wistfully, but truthfully enough anyway.

"Bull- Bull- Bull-oney."

The token bag had properly faded out of sight. The last odor of z's presence must have finally dissipated.

"Check please," I was having as much fun as a man can ever expect to have before ten in the a.m., but I had some place to be. And miles to go before I leaped. Flashed. Leaped on the darkest evening of the year. Solstice. Frost.

"Now don't take it so much to heart," she said as she batted her heavily mascaraed eyelashes. False for sure. "You evil ones don't mind giving it out, but taking it's another thing."

She knows all about taking it, that's for sure.

I didn't feel the cold when I stepped outside. Even without the gin, the whiskey, the...fucking vodka. I had the warm coat on.

What I did feel when I stepped outside was the danger. The heightened sense that someone was in trouble.

I went around back, and there, sheltered by the garbage bins and a stand of trees, was Eloise laid out on a tarp with a three-hundred-pound trucker doing his best to get something started with her, but it was cold and the glow-plugs had a hard time getting to the right temperature.

"Don't just stand there, you prick," Eloise said, "help!"

Now in a different situation, I might have had to consider what kind of help she wanted. Perhaps she needed something on the other end. But the panicked look in her eyes, not to mention the urgent squeak of her voice, corroborated my sense of danger.

Before she had finished asking for help, the bag had already re-appeared, and the dagger was in my hand. The dagger. You've seen it. T.E. Lawrence posed for a photo while wearing it. The caption said the dagger was a gift from Emir Faisal of Arabia. But it was my dagger. The photographer in Essex thought it would be a good prop. T.E. and I had covered some good ground, taking full advantage of the justification of the White Man's Burden (thank you, Rudyard) to wreck havoc on the generally backward folk of the rest of the world.

The dagger was in my hand, unsheathed, just as the trucker unsheathed his weapon. But the dagger plunged home long before the trucker had time to plunge anything, either home or away. I split him from liver to spleen, and the blubber and warm organs issued forth and steamed in the dirty snow under the trees in God's country.

Maybe I had made a too-hasty analysis of Eloise when I first noticed her. Which is to say, maybe I had not noticed her at all. Merely another fungible waitress in a fungible truck stop in a fungible place in this very fungible world of worlds.

But as I helped her to her feet, no worse for the trucker fucker's wear, she seemed to transform into a goddess. No, I swear I hadn't had anything to drink. You don't know how these things work. Maybe that is what helped convince me.

"Took you long enough," was all she said as she mussed her hair and straightened her over-starched uniform.

"You weren't exactly screaming. In this part of the world you could have brought the whole town in with a hefty shout from those healthy lungs. Or maybe you already cried wolf too many times?"

"I'm not talking about today, you idiot. I've been here a week waiting for you."

"I don't get it," I said. Something strange was going on. This flash had started off on the wrong foot and now moved to the worst foot.

"You don't get it. I got that message, cupcake. You don't get it. Get in the truck and you'll hear all about it until you get it, and once you get it, you'll have wished you never had."

I checked her over for signs of yellow ochre clothing. The maroon diner's uniform looked safe enough, but you could never tell what was underneath.

"I can't be too careful this close to the flash. You know what you need to do," I told her.

She knew. She knew all right. She knew, but she didn't like it. If she really was who she was showing herself to be, she would do it without being asked.

"No touching," she said.

I waited.

She stripped. Black bra. Black panties...with the little red bow.

She hesitated. She had been stationed here long enough to acquire a measure of modesty.

Then off came the undergarments. No tattoos. No yellow ochre tattoos anywhere. I examined every inch, and was satisfied that she was not the one I feared she could have been. The one with the yellow ochre tattoo on her left hip.

"I'm not her and you know it."

"No. I must say you are not."

"Disappointed?"

"Intrigued."

"Short of time too. You don't know what shit's coming down. Neither did z. Let's get going."

Three truckers came out of the cafe and saw Eloise pulling on her uniform.

"Hey, buddy, did you save some for us?"

The men approached my truck.

"What you do to Billy?" the tall, nervous one shouted in shock when he spotted the lump of flesh.

The fat man in the red flannel hunting shirt pulled a revolver that he had tucked in the small of his back.

I had the ignition on and was already speeding into reverse when Eloise jumped in. Her door slammed shut when I braked hard. I slammed the transmission into drive.

A bullet took out the back window, but missed the soft tissue of human flesh, particularly two heads in the truck. How it failed to take out the front window too, I'll never know. We never did look for the slug, but then we didn't care too much to look for it either. We had other things on our minds.

More shots filled the air, like at a redneck Fourth of July ball, but we were out of danger, speeding north on U.S. 95, saying so long to Moscow. Moscow, Idaho, that is.

* * *

Moscow, Russia, on the other hand, now that has its own story.

I had specifically asked for an assignment where I could study French poetry. I guess they were sending me a message about my choice of hobby by sending me as a woman. This was in 1831. Czarist Russia, as I said before. And they sent me as the damn wife of one Alexander Pushkin, brightest star of the non-French poetry firmament. They weren't always on the ball when it came to assignments, but when they were on top of things they could show you a thing or two about how to wield a devastating sense of humor.

To this day, I can't read Rimbaud. I lived through my own season in hell, and if their purpose was to denude me of my *je ne sais qua*, it worked.

But damn that z. I have never been able to figure that creature out.

My dearest Alex had been exiled for writing naughty ditties about the Czar. He was exiled on his mother's estate in Pskov, about twelve miles from the Estonian border. Now, if you are going to be exiled within the boundaries of Russia, twelve miles from the Estonian border isn't the worst of places to be. I mean, compared to the miserable possibilities of, oh, nearly the entire northern half of the continent of Asia, even then commonly referred to as *Siberia*, mom's country home not far from St. Pete's was heaven.

But being officially exiled, they refused to publish both *Boris Gudenov* and *Eugene Onegin*. If you happen to only now learn that Boris and Eugene are works of literature and not Alex's drinking buddies, then you can be comforted to know that Boris and Eugene have just found it out for themselves too. They are pleased to know they can now be published.

After a few years of exile, dearest Alex was granted permission to travel to Moscow to immolate himself (metaphorically speaking, that is—he was a brilliant poet after all, though not a French poet, otherwise he would have said *immoler*, but he wasn't French, and didn't know how to conjugate the verb, *immoler*, so he had to settle for *immolate* even though he didn't speak English either, but he could use it because by special dispensation from the powers that be (were) for about thirty years around this time, the Russian word for *immolate* happened to be *immolate*, even in Cyrillic), in front of Czar Nicolas I, Santa's nephew, and beg for somewhat of a pardon.

Moscow. And damn it all if it wasn't *z* posing as the French poet, Georges-Charles de Heeckeren d'Anthès. And damn it all even more if *z* didn't seduce me. I could blame the six years of estrogen that had been coursing through my veins by that time, but on the other hand I've always wondered about *z*. I mean, mister, misses, miss, monsieur, Madame, mademoiselle, monsignor, mss, you just can't be sure about him/her/it. Maybe it wasn't such a funny thing after all.

And the poetry. Pure French. Perhaps it was a bone they were throwing my way for my suffering under their sophomoric joke, but I did get my six months of French poetry education after all, even if it was from z. I simply closed my eyes and pretended, just as all women learn to do at one time or another.

Well, the rumors of my *ménage* reached Alex—before we left Moscow, but after he had secured the Czar's permission to publish *Boris* and *Eugene*. Alex challenged Georges-Charles to a duel. You wouldn't believe the rush it is having two gentlemen fight a duel over your honor! And of course, George-Charles (nee z) gave Alex what for. Alex let George-Charles shoot first, not realizing the advantage George-Charles had in a laser-sighted sniper rifle. Alex simply laughed because he thought it was a kind of cotton gin. Technology always gives an edge in mortal combat, whether it is *mano-a-mano*, or global thermonuclear annihilation. Two days later, the world's foremost poet was dead.

Yes, two days.

George-Charles, despite the technological advantage, had merely grazed poor Alex, but the wound became infected with a twenty-first century bacterium that had attached itself to the slug during its manufacture two centuries later in, of all places, Pskov (everyone was friends by then). Alex had no immunity to such bacteria, and that was that. Alex was dead. But that was okay, because as I said, he wasn't French.

Boris went off with Natasha to hunt down flying squirrels and talking Meese, and Eugene, feeling his name was too gay for nineteenth-century Russia, ran off to the Pacific Northwest of the United States of America where he became a socially progressive logging town replete with lumber and lawyers, pot holes and pot heads.

Georges-Charles ran off with the male lead of the Bolshoi Ballet, and I still never figured out what exactly *z* was or wasn't—is or isn't. Like I said, I had closed my eyes and pretended.

I lived out my assignment with my four children (I still haven't gotten rid of the stretch marks and cellulose) on their grandmother's estate twelve miles from the Estonian border. I wrote French poetry, translated it into Russian, and published it as "unpublished" manuscripts from my dearly departed and long-lost Alex. The critics noticed the improvement.

Then the bastards finally set me free and gave me back my full complement of chromosomes, both the X's *and* the Y's, and put me on a mountaintop in Tennessee.

* * *

"I knew a girl named Heloise once. She spelled it with an aitch," I said. The junction with the secondary highway into the mountains was fast approaching, and we were approaching it almost as fast.

"Bullshit," Eloise said. She looked out her passenger-side window at the still-rising sun. "Half the stuff you claim to have seen or done is total fabrication. I've read the files in your Permanent Record."

"But the half that's true could fill a book."

"You were never Abelard, so don't pull that lover-boy game with me. I eat boys like you for breakfast."

"No, I wasn't Abelard. It's true. But I did know Heloise," I hated the serious turn this conversation was taking, but maybe it had to do with the roadblocks and the mass of protesters blocking the junction.

"I knew her too. It's why I took her name for this assignment."

"Why did you drop the aitch?"

"To spite professor 'enry 'iggins. I made it to the church on time, but he—," she swallowed hard, "Keep on the highway, don't turn off."

"It's our turn-off to the flash point."

Eloise turned and looked at me with her black, moist eyes. She was no longer the goddess, but she was not the trailer tramp I had first known her to be either. She was a nice-looking, all-American girl, a touch of Hilary Clinton with a hint of Sarah Palin.

"Don't you see who those protesters are?"

"The banner says, 'Occupy Viola!'"

"And their coats are what color?"

"I see your point," I pressed on the gas and blew by the yellow-ochre-clad protesters as they brought down the evil forces of Wall Street from the ramparts of Main Street.

"Goddamn z was way off. Shit. The fucker."

"You catch a case of tourette's on your entry flash, El?"

"Mitch, you don't know how serious it is."

I really didn't like the double-serious turn this conversation was taking.

"I know. I touched the Void last time," I lamented. "z said they had some sort of punishment in store for me."

"You're just a naughty little boy, aren't you? And z told you the first flash point is all you get this time?"

"Yeah," This girl knew too damn much about everything.

"He had it upside-down and inside-out. The fact is, the first and second flash points are already dissolved. You only have the third flash point available. It's your last and only chance. And it's my job to make sure you get there."

I looked at my GPS. Still Bombay.

"Forget that bundle of crackerjack, Magellan."

"So you are saying the flash point up in the Palouse Range is out?"

"And so is the secondary in Bombay," she said, pointing to my precious device.

"Where are we going?"

"You ever hear of the Brooks Range?" Her eyes threw daggers. Liquid daggers of remorse and dread.

My heart sank.

"Alaska?"

She gave me one curt nod and pursed her lips.

"Winter Solstice in fucking Alaska?"

"Has to be above the Arctic Circle. No light. You don't know what shit is going on up above—or down below."

"All because I touched the Void?"

"Fuck you, diva boy. You touched the Void and you think heaven and hell is so sensitive to crumble at your little violation of the rules? Your little prank, your idyll, your frolic?"

"What are you so worked up about?" I said. "We have two days and a couple hours on top of that to make it. It will be tight, but it's not impossible."

Eloise was irritated. "Goddamn it, it's my fault, okay? That's why I'm so fucking worked up. You think you're so special for touching the Void?" Eloise spat at me. "Well I entered it! I entered the Void, and now I'm the one who has to set things right by getting you out of here before you and all the rest of our agents are sealed in time forever."

I couldn't look into her face. I was driving, but I had been watching the road and her eyes alternately. Now I looked at the road and her tits alternately. She had transformed her waitress uniform into jeans and a tight-fitting long-sleeved turtleneck. Her tits didn't make me feel as pathetic as her eyes did.

"Is it really that bad?" I asked her tits. Then I looked at the road and waited for a reply.

"It's worse. To pull this off—to get you where you need to be—I must sacrifice my life."

I haven't cried in three incarnations, but I felt a knot in my gut and catch in my throat. My eyes became sodden. Damn capital punishment.

"That's worst-case, right?"

"I've seen the permutations. I die in one hundred percent of the scenarios."

I thought to ask her for a token of her authority. Taking me off-course from z's instructions with such a maudlin and dramatic explanation was exactly something I'd expect from the trenchies. But something told me she was authentic. Maybe it was that knot in my gut. Something touched me deeply. Then again, that might have just been the *huevos rancheros* from the diner.

"If you're thinking about some token of authority, how about this?"

Eloise handed me the device.

I looked into her eyes again.

It was the missing token. The token I thought I had lost thanks to z's clumsy appearance.

My astrolabe.

"I know you weren't Abelard in that incarnation. You were Astrolabe," Eloise said, looking far into the horizon ahead. I could not fathom what she could be seeing. "I was a sister under your mother when she was abbess of the Oratory of the Paraclete."

My mother. Not my mother. Astrolabe's mother. I was only Astrolabe from twenty to forty-five years. The eternal question remained: Who was my mother?

"I know what you're thinking," she said.

I was still trying to process the heavy load she had dropped on my doorstep. I simply looked at her tits then her eyes then her tits again. Then the road. I am a good driver. A good driver with the naughtiest, strangest, most wonderful girl I'd ever met as my passenger.

"Oh really?" I said. "So what am I thinking?"

She smirked and said, "You're thinking if it's true that I'm going to die, then you won't have to use a condom when the inevitable happens somewhere along our journey."

Damn, that woman knows me too well.

Chapter 3

"How about this?" I asked.

Eloise stared down into her coffee as she responded. "I'm not into that kind of kinky sex."

I thought again. "This?"

"Definitely not," Eloise said. "Too much Fluid. This is really getting tiresome, Mitch."

I picked up another couple lamb fries from the plate, plunged them into the creamy ranch dressing, and tossed them in my mouth. "*You* think it's tiresome. Try having dinner with someone who can read your mind."

"Fuck off," she said. "That's not a nice thought, Mitch."

Alaska through Canada was no good. I was glad, actually. I hate their beer and hockey, although curling is another story entirely.

We'd driven through the morning into the afternoon and had to turn back south just sixty miles outside Coeur d'Alene. The rapid and geometrical increase in yellow ochre clothes, trucks, animals—you get me—was just too much of a clue, even for me. I also knew a thing or two about borders and border agents. Was a specialty of mine ever since Prussia. But, that's another thing altogether.

"Maybe," Eloise began. "we can get passage on a ship. From one of the west coast ports."

We now sat in the *Lucky 13* Bar in Potlatch. I'd decided earlier that I hadn't been on a bender for a while. Today was my lucky day. I tried to flag down our waitress, an attractive twenty-something blond in a pair of jeans that'd been spray painted on her and a white button down shirt that barely held back the load of her…

"She's more a thirty-something," Eloise said. "She's not really blond, either. Look at her roots. They're brunette. She thinks you're gay because you're ignoring me."

Like I said, we are in this bar, ducking the trenchies until we come up with Plan B, which considering Plan A was a total failure…

"Plan A was working just fine," she said. "Until you killed that truck driver."

"Would you stop that!" I said. I turned. "Waitress! Another round for me. Please. Thank you."

My back was killing me. In each incarnation, the backaches always start when I turn forty-two. I bent forward in the cramped booth, slamming my knee directly into the table leg.

"Fuck!" I said. "That hurt."

Eloise met my eyes. She had a different look now. One which reminded me of a time when I'd been a part of something more than me, more than a brief.

"I can't read you anymore," Eloise said. "Raw emotions. Creates a fog I can't get through."

"Finally," I said. "A weakness."

"Give me some time. I'll figure it out."

"I need to ask you something, Eloise."

She nodded. "Sure. Non sequitur award of the day."

"Glenda," I said. "The waitress. In Moscow. Back at the diner. Called me the 'Evil One' this morning as I was leaving. Does she know?"

"Your drink, sir," came my waitress's angelic voice from above me. I turned to her and took the glass.

Eloise was right. Definitely not a blond. "Thanks, honey. More coffee, sis?" the waitress asked.

Eloise covered her cup. "I'm fine."

Our waitress gave me a big smile. "Let me know if you need anything else."

She sashayed away from our table.

I leaned back in the booth. "Am I good or what?"

"Ha!" Eloise said. "Now she thinks you're too old and probably have a small dick."

"Dammit!"

Eloise looked out the singlewide window of the bar. It was late in the afternoon. My second day was wearing and growing old. She ran her forefinger around the lip of the coffee mug. "'Evil One.' Are you serious Mitch? You don't seem to be the archetype for a follower of that sect. I doubt dear Glenda had any idea what she was implying. I'm surprised. Didn't take you for a believer."

"Who says I am?" I said. "Just makes you wonder. With what we do and all."

"It's all mythological bullshit," Eloise said.

"Still," I said. "It's an exact term."

"What are you thinking?"

"Their return. What else?"

"You can't be serious. Prime Movers?" Eloise laughed. "The Gathering and Dissolution? You've been here too long, Mitch. That's all fairy tale shit. You know it. "

"Ever channel an indirect?" I said.

Eloise was quiet for a long time before she answered. "Another black mark for you, Mitch."

"African American mark, Eloise. Come on. Get with the times. I felt the Flow!"

"Still doesn't mean you can use an indirect! And I do mean use! What the hell is wrong with you?"

"It works both directions. The enlightenment of it. Like a drug. I've been channeling an indirect the last ten years! You can see both ways! Touching the Void opened it to me."

"The Void!" Eloise said as she slid out of the booth and stood up. "You have no idea what you're fucking with. Look. I've got to make a few calls. Find a way out of here before it's too late."

"That's good," I said getting out of the booth. "I've got to take a piss. But, you know that already."

"Ha, ha," Eloise said.

I found the men's room next to the kitchen, giving the fake-blond waitress a slap on the ass as I walked by. Small dick. Whatever.

"Really small," Eloise yelled. "Got that Mitch?"

I passed into the bathroom. I stood in front of the urinal and settled into a nice piss. The one where it just drains from you. With not a hint of asparagus.

"Note, Mitch. Inebriation doesn't keep our foe at bay. Just blinds them. For a while."

"Shit, z," I said. "Would you stop sneaking up on me? Two visits from you in the same incarnation? I must be special."

z moved in front of the urinal next to mine. "If you stay much longer in this bar, you're going to miss your primary flash point. If you're lost, I'll give you a clue. It's near the Route of the Hiawatha Bike Trail. Just take that, and you're home."

"I know where it is," I said.

"You're not on the shores of the Gitche Gummee, my dear fellow," z said. "You don't believe that woman, do you?"

"Eloise? Why shouldn't I?"

"Poppycock!" z said. "Absolute rubbish! Let me guess. She returned a token, yes?"

"She can read my thoughts."

"Of course she can read thoughts!" z said. "She entered the Void! She's now a Special. An example for you of what not to do. Mark me, Mitch. You take care. The fireworks haven't even begun yet."

"I think she's telling the truth."

z zipped up. "Truth? (a laugh) Truth? I am surprised, Mitch. We *make* the Truth! You still don't get it. Poor Mitch. Can't wrap that minuscule mind of yours around it."

"I think we're done here, z," I said.

"Look, Mitch," z said. "Histrionics, at its core elemental state is about one thing: the rejection of Absolute Truth. You know this; it was covered thoroughly in the elementary classes. We tend to lose sight of the real power of this simple, dare I say, Truth."

"What about the indirects?"

z really laughed. "Interesting thought problem. We've had this discussion. I do not concern myself with indirects. After a while, you won't either."

z walked to the sink and washed. "A Special. Of all things. On my watch, too. That's why you must make your primary flash point. To reset this woman. She's infected you, Mitch. You'll think she's a Prime Mover before too much long-er…that was a joke."

"She told me the primary and suckie have dissolved. I'm overdue."

z threw the paper towel in the trash and turned to me. "Mitch. Do the right thing, yes? Do what you're here for. Make your primary flash point. It *is* your brief, understand? That's a good boy. Make your flash. Make your jump. Make it poetic. Make it French. Make it your last stand. Remember the Alamo. Remember Knoxville, right? Of course I'm right."

Last stand. Didn't I know it.

Knoxville. 1836. As z would say *like so many leaves of grass, right?*

Of course I'm right.

* * *

The Alamo.

I remember it well. Was just like yesterday.

I had awoken. There had been voices around me. Spanish. American. No French this time.

"He's coming back!"

"Thought he was dead."

I'd been gut shot, and I have never felt such pain. Under certain circumstances, they flashed you into a body that was on the verge of death. I know, raises all of the morality questions. But, I don't do ethics.

"Didn't think he'd pull through," another voice said. "Crockett said he was a goner."

The pain in my gut was deafening.

"Shit! Crockett's dead! This boy is a miracle."

"Shut up all of you! He's coming around."

I had fluttered my eyes.

My shape was finally fully formed in this body.

The jump was complete. The burn of the flash was gone.

I had known flashing in that he wasn't a Walker. Could tell by the terror he had been undergoing, the raw emotion fucking with the remnants as I'd tried to place myself in the body. *His body.*

"Better get those boots of his back to him, Isaiah."

Apparently, I had been a backwoodsmen and sharp shooter. A veteran and miracle survivor of the Alamo. I go by the name of Jebediah T. Jefferson.

Jefferson, of all things.

Jebediah's Jefferson lineage in the States had been started by Mary Jane Maryton, a Pilgrim heretic who'd stowed away on the *Mayflower* and had been willingly de-flowered en route. She'd taken 'Jefferson' as her missing husband's surname by accident.

Let me explain. Shift change. It's when we're the most vulnerable as Walkers. The scuttlebutt I'd heard said that while the *Mayflower* had been en route to the New World, Mary had flashed onto the ship from her last brief in 1776 Philadelphia. She'd failed to clear the jump remnants. Typical rookie mistake, but there you are. The more I have to deal with these kinds of fuck-ups, the more I think those who direct my work could do with a shake up.

Don't even get me started on the now infamous Barabbas screw up, which was one of my first Time Walker assignments. I did get a really cool cup out of it.

In any event, Mary's inadvertent name selection had created the beginning of a long line of second-rate Jefferson's, all of whom implied an intimate connection with Big T.J. when his star would rise a century later.

You never hear about Mary Jefferson in the history books (I'll get back to this oxymoron) because she had been Bradford's bitch, who had ghost written most of his junk, including that *Plantation* rag, which despite mom's attempts, never passed for writing. Quality writing, that is, and isn't that all that authors ever do? I digress, however. And they say Bradford's wife had accidentally 'fallen' off the *Mayflower* while he had been out scouting. Right.

Alas, back to Tennessee. Back to my Alamo brief.

After I'd healed from my wounds and made the odyssey from the destruction of the Alamo to Tennessee, I had arrived home in Knoxville early summer of 1836. I had discovered I was married to Belle, a twenty-two-year-old pistol of a woman who had been the French teacher at the ladies' school in Knoxville. Before going to Texas to fight with Crockett, I'd drug her up into the mountains, had my way with her, and put a ring on her finger.

From the first night of my return, Belle had known that Jebediah wasn't Jebediah. She commented on the improvement of her conjugal situation, too. We never conceived a child. Belle. My poor Belle.

The Jefferson name did get me a few drinks here and there. More importantly, the name had helped me establish my young man's enterprise: *Distillation of Spirits Both Powerful and Medicinal, with emphasis on the Ladies' Calmer*. My special brew, special concoction. My gift to humanity.

Ended up selling my stake in the business to Jasper before jumping out. Even came up with the three-stage still. All of this illegal, of course.

As chance would have it, *z* had shown up the day of my twentieth wedding anniversary. Timing is everything, *z* had said. *z* had been resplendent in his costume. *z* loved period pieces and this was a favorite. I must admit, *z* did fit the bill to a tee.

"You're going native on this one," *z* had said. "Eventually happens to the best agents."

"Thanks," I'd said, shocked by his statement.

"I offered no compliment," *z* had said. "I meant I'm surprised it happened to *you*."

I ignored him.

"Is that the time?" *z* asked. "I must go. Have a meeting with Jasper. Some business venture I'm involved with. No. I'm not at liberty to discuss the details with you. You need to get going, Mitch."

Before Knoxville, I hadn't questioned, morally or otherwise, the Assumption. For a Walker, you can't. It's anathema to the job, to the brief. How else do you flash in but assume the form of someone who is already there? In my case, it's usually another Walker working the infant to twenty-year-old shift so you kind of tag in as they tag out like some kind of cosmic professional wrestling event only without the steroids and leotards. I had had my fill of wrestling, both on and off the field of play, in Greece during the first Olympics, thank you very much.

But this time, I'd assumed a corpse. It seemed simple, yet complex. It's all timing even though time doesn't mean anything to me anymore. Time is boredom, trying to find a way to get through twenty-five years of the monotony of the brief before you punch out. But with Belle there was something new. Something different.

The trenchies had begun showing up when I had turned forty. Thought I'd been imagining them. I saw the hints of ochre though. The Manifold isn't perfect and does have cracks, which is how those fuckers can get in early.

My day had finally come on a warm spring day in 1856. I had packed and had said goodbye to Belle. Somehow, she had known I wasn't coming back.

Regrets? I have a few. We all do, I imagine. Have moved past them, since. I visit Belle's grave in Knoxville when the time frame of my incarnation allows, not that that means anything. Just dealing with loose ends.

Then, I flashed and was gone from Knoxville. I awoke in the Time Closet.

That's bad, by the way.

* * *

z left the bathroom.

I shook, tucked in, and zipped up before heading back into the bar.

The waitress shot me another smile. I ignored it. *Let the line run out a bit on this one if you want to set the hook,* as Papa would have said.

I returned to the table. Empty. Eloise had left her coat.

I slid into the booth and waited.

"John's love for God…" I muttered. That's what the minister had said. Hard to believe John's funeral was just a day ago. He'd be in the ground by now.

Entropy and mundane existence. We all bear it, even me. The problem was, I have this tendency to fuck off during my shift, like most people do. The bigger problem is that my fuck-offs can be a decade long.

I just get distracted, that's all. Something comes along and pulls my attention this way, or her way, and before I know it, a decade has gone by. It hits me usually when I'm around thirty-two. I tend to go on a self-imposed sabbatical for eight or nine years. Strictly business, of course.

Time Walker is something of a misnomer: sounds all cool and shit, but the brass tacks of it always comes down to my third rule of the infiniteverse: life is really fucking boring.

John knew this, became aware of it as we 'togethered.' He learned from my aura to the point I'd infected him. For ten years, he had been an indirect; *my indirect*. A conduit of my experiences and knowledge. You run across one every hundred jumps or so. John was my tenth; you do the math.

I rattled the token bag, found John's Naval Academy ring, and pulled it out. What is a token but a fixture in a certain place and time? A device you use to recreate what was in the here and now? But does it work? Does it? I've jumped over a thousand times. I still don't get it. The flash. The purpose.

I looked around the bar. No sign of Eloise. She was in the head most likely. The late afternoon pre-Solstice sun hugged the horizon. Soon. All too soon.

I returned my attention to John's ring. As I've said, I'd missed the primary a few times. Not for any reason in particular. Sometimes it's lack of attention on my part. I just forgot it was coming. You risk the shift when your primary flash point dissolves. Depending on how those who direct my work arranged the Manifold on that jump, I get a time add-on if I miss my primary. A bonus, if you will.

They know me all too well. I used to miss the primary a lot because of the extras. They get pissed when they find out. The second and third points are for emergencies only, not for extra duty-free shopping, as it were.

"Fuck 'em" had been my response to z.

The end result is a viable Manifold-arranged incarnation where you get the shift for each flash point you miss. It's automatic. The powers that be don't have time to diddle in each incarnation. Believe me, I know. In other words, I get anywhere from a few days to a week to make my auxiliary flash points if I miss the primary.

"Your first flash point is your brief," z had said. I don't see what z went on about. It's not a big deal. If the first and second flash points are gone, then I have about seven days to make it to Alaska. Apparently, there is some kind of physics behind this.

But, I'm not Tech. I've got enough to do each incarnation without worrying about the dimensional stability, let alone time harmonics, of that particular Manifold. Yeah, I paid attention in class.

A flash of yellow ochre from outside the bar caught my attention. I looked out the bar's wide window.

Eloise, in my truck, the gravel of the parking lot a-flying as she pulled my rig out onto Onaway Road, heading west to Highway 6 in the red burn of the late December setting sun.

Like a trenchie out of Hell.

I thought a really bad thought before she was out of range.

"And I mean it!" I yelled.

Chapter 4

Three. There were three of them. Three squad cars raced past me with their sirens in full throat.

I hope they kill the bitch.

In each squad car sat three deputies. Had to be the entire peacekeeping force of central Idaho.

Damn. Why'd she have to do that? I was just starting to like her.

I'd had enough of the bars and diners and lounges. I'd had enough of my protected places against the yellow-ochre trenchies. But I could feel them closing in on me the longer I stood outside with my jock around my ankles, so to speak. To speak. Perchance to dream.

I checked the parking lot for any kind of car I could hot-wire. It was unnecessary. The pea-soup-colored Ford Pinto with the faux wood-grained side panels idled nearby without a driver. Without a passenger. Without any of God's creatures in it whatsoever. Something wasn't right, though. Too easy. I backed away when I smelled it. The yellow ochre. I don't have the best olfactory sensibilities, but when the entire interior is decked out in yellow ochre fabric, even I can't help but notice it.

I'm not returning to that damn diner. I gotta get to my flash point or out of Idaho altogether.

Two drunks stumbled out of the diner blurbling about a killer on the loose. So the trucker who had been molesting Eloise wasn't a trenchie after all. It's not the first time I've killed a human. I wouldn't say I'm proud of it, but I can say with a clear conscience that only those who deserved it ever got it. Except maybe in Dresden. But that was war. That was duty. *Duty's Dance with Death,* so the story goes.

I was flight attendant for a certain famous bombing run the night of Valentine's Day, 1945. Love was in the air. To hear the crew talk about it, the greatest tragedy of the night was when I ran out of the packets of peanuts and had to break open the emergency packets of stale pretzels.

We had clear instructions to avoid the slaughterhouse at all costs. Later, when the generals discovered that those instructions had preserved the one person who had the talent, the skill, the means, and the balls to tell the world the truth about that three-day campaign, they vowed never again to be so discriminating in their planning. All or nothing was their motto. And they took their motto with them on the re-assignment to the Pacific where they set their sights on southern Japan. I was not on the Enola Gay, so don't even try to hang that one on me.

But yeah, I've had my share of killing. Humans, that is. When they've deserved it. Well, you don't have to buy it. We all justify our deeds as we see fit. But didn't you see what he was doing to that bitch? And see what thanks I get? Might as well have stabbed me in the back for saving her sorry ass from that fat hairy ape. I'm sorry, do I sound bitter? Okay, I can fall into self-pity as well as any human can.

Trenchies are nothing on my conscience. Kill 'em and you're doing everyone a favor. Even them. But a human, you gotta deal with that law enforcement crap. As if trying to get to my flash point, whichever one I was supposed to get to that is, wasn't difficult enough what with the yellow-ochre menace gathering around me.

My truck was gone, and that meant so too was all my equipment.

My tent!

Even if I throw my lot in with *z* and stick with the first flash point, I would need to re-stock the standard equipment and supplies that I had so carefully gathered the past few weeks.

Across the highway sat a lonely building. No big box store here in this neck of the woods. The small brick building had been a mercantile in the old days. Now it appeared to be a hardware store. Butch's Hardware was what the faded sign had grown weary of touting. I could find any car to hijack, but it's tough to hijack a tent. Not enough of them lying around.

Better go buy one fair and square.

I crossed the highway without incident. You'd have to be a Time Walker to appreciate how important that is this close to a flash, especially when all Moscow is breaking loose.

The door to the hardware store squeaked when I opened it, and it struck something metallic. I looked up to find a bell that couldn't tinkle. The clapper had fallen out of it long ago.

Apparently the squeak of the door and the dull clunk on the broken bell wasn't enough to wake the proprietor. Two-to-one the guy's name wasn't Butch.

At first I didn't know if I'd entered a taxidermist shop or a hardware store. Maybe it was both. Deer, antelope, ducks, bear, bison, and even an elephant head adorned the dim, dusty interior of this less-than-thriving enterprise. The word *grotesquerie* came to mind. Like French poetry. But in the aisles were the standard fare for such wasteland hardware stores. Nails, barbed wire, gopher traps, and girlie magazines.

I approached the sleeping proprietor. His head was on the counter near the old cash register. Only it wasn't a he. It was a gnarled old woman who reminded me of a school cafeteria lunch lady. She snored. And I was wrong. Her nametag showed that her name *was* Butch. You should have taken me up on those odds.

I let her sleep it off. Who knows what kind of geriatric rave party she had attended the night before.

Under the calendar with the large photo of Miss Idaho, 1954 (was it Butch?), was a pup tent set up as a display model. It sat on an eight-by-ten rectangle of green artificial grass and had a little wooden picket fence made out of kindling neatly arranged around it.

The best thing of all was no hint of yellow ochre. Nowhere in the store. So I thought, what the hell?

I crawled inside the tent and pulled the mirror out of my token bag. Worst that could happen was *z* would find me and tell me to get to work.

Something worse than the worst that could happen happened.

* * *

They had thought they were doing me a favor, sending me back to the dawn of human evolution. Hazing was more like it. *z* insists it was on the up and up, but I told him up his and up Aunt Jenny's too as far as I was concerned.

Sending a newbie back to the dawn of human evolution didn't do anything for me, and I've never been able to argue the professors of anthropology out of their earnest but way off the mark characterizations of pre-*homo sapiens*. *Homo Erectus* was a man's man, and as human as any other, only more erect. They had not yet figured out they had to publish the warnings during football and golf broadcasts that anyone who was erect for more than four hours should see a doctor.

They were always erect. No little blue pills required.

The problem was that the great creator forgot to create *Homo Sappho* as a complementary being to help reproduce the race. So after the first batch of *Homo Erectus* died off, the world was left to the more flexible species of human, *Homo Sapiens*. All my other incarnations as a human have been as *Homo Sapiens*, except that first one. I have nothing to say about my incarnations as a non-human. You wouldn't understand. No, *z* is right. You would understand. I just never learned to communicate in non-human languages. It's why I got stuck with this gig at the low end of the great chain of being.

I have no regrets—as long as *z* isn't around to mock me about it. After all, that was where I met John. Big John Johnson we called him at the time. You get the picture.

My primary duty was to introduce fire to these wayward folks, and I must say they were very thankful. But they only had one way to show their gratitude. After the first week I went off to the Cave of Solitude and let them show their gratitude to each other.

The Cave of Solitude is where I met John. Big John Johnson. He asked how I liked the new job.

"I've been had," I said.

He just smiled at me with a knowing smile, but he said nothing. I know he was in on the joke. But no one has yet admitted it outright.

I made plenty of rookie mistakes, but I guess they figured I couldn't screw things up way back at the beginning of time. Human time that is. *z* as much as admitted, though, that if they had known Chaos Theory that far back, they wouldn't have sent their fresh graduates on first assignments to what turned out to be an important period in history.

"Small changes in initial conditions, my love," *z* said, "Can lead to large differences in resulting states. If only we had known! You neophytes delayed by half a million years the Iron Age, Bronze Age, Gilded Age, and Information Age, not to mention the twenty-second-century Sex Age."

I smiled and told z that without us, such ages could have been delayed another million years.

You know when z knows he's wrong. He doesn't say anything. He was careful about what he admitted about the machinations of the inner sanctum from then on—unless he's just looking for someone on whom he can unload his bitchiness about Aunt Jenny.

The Cave of Solitude. John. He taught me how to share solitude with another. Such paradoxes are not beyond the grasp of a Time Walker.

Then z joined, and it was no longer the Cave of Solitude. It was the Cave of Three. Then z kicked us in the ass and told us to get to work ingratiating ourselves with the *Homo Erectus* humans. We returned to the happy men and made another fire. They were grateful again. Much to our discomfort.

z and Aunt Jenny chuckled through the whole twenty-five years.

* * *

Butch's Hardware store was not my flash point, no matter how much I wanted it to be. The mirror was blank. Not blank, it was simple glass. I looked through it and contemplated my shoes.

Then Butch put her head into the flap of the tent and said, "There he is."

"There who is?" I asked.

Another round, elderly face, a man this time—named Shirley no doubt—put his head into the flap of the tent. Two moons looked at me with salacious grins.

"What have we here?" Shirley asked.

Only the man was not named Shirley. He was Irene. And he was not just a man, he was a sheriff's deputy. And he was not just a sheriff's deputy, he was a sheriff's deputy with a yellow-ochre badge.

My sphincter tightened. I thought of John.

But instead of annihilating me, as most trenchies were out to do, Deputy Irene invited me to leave the tent. He said his relationship with Butch had taught him valuable lessons regarding humankind, and he wanted to extend his salacious compassion to even the Time Walker he was instructed to obliterate.

My sphincter relaxed. I thought of John.

I stepped out of the tent. I felt like a boy. I tried to think about my mother, but I drew a blank.

"What will you do with him, Irene?" Butch asked the Deputy.

"I will spirit him off to the Brooks Range where his destiny and mine awaits."

Brooks Range? Eloise. Goddamn bitch. She's in league with them.

Irene removed his sheriff's hat and kissed Butch hard on the lips. I turned my eyes when he probed her dentures with his tongue.

A black and white television behind the counter broadcast a news flash. A man had turned himself in as the killer of the trucker outside the Moscow diner. Even on the black and white screen, I could tell the man's t-shirt was yellow ochre.

Irene looked at me.

"Our bosses sacrificed one of us to get the pigs off your track," Irene said.

"Not for my benefit, I'm sure," I replied.

"For theirs. The Palouse Range is out of the picture now. But I'll help you get to the Brooks Range."

I wasn't going to ask for an explanation. He'd likely lie to me like every other Irene I have ever known has lied to me.

He was anxious to tell. "I'm sick of it. Too much drama behind the scenes, you know? Everyone looking to slip through the Manifold and get a Time Walker so we get off the cusp of oblivion."

I was silent. He would talk.

"Butch has helped me see that I'm more likely to find redemption by helping a Time Walker than by trying to bring one down."

"What does Butch know about the infiniteverse?" I asked. My curiosity had gotten the best of me and I had entered the conversation.

"Nothing," Irene said. Butch confirmed this with a shake of her head and a vacuous look in her eyes. "She's just a good egg with a heart of gold."

That wasn't exactly the turn of phrase that met my literary standards, but Irene likely hadn't surveyed the literature of hundreds of civilizations and species either. So I cut him a break.

"Let's go," Irene said.

My sphincter tightened. *John.*

"You coming, Butch?" Irene asked.

"I must mind my store, Irene," Butch said.

"We need three," Irene answered.

"Why three?" Butch asked.

"It's the magic number," Irene answered.

"It sounds dangerous," Butch said, worriedly.

"I'll come visit you when I've completed my mission," Irene said.

"Oh, Irene! My hero!" Butch drooled.

Irene led me from the store. A semi sped by on the highway. Black letters splashed across the trailer read, "The Man in the Dark Trench Coat."

My sphincter tightened even more. I thought about *Homo Erectus.*

At the van, Irene let me enter the passenger side. He held the door for me, real gentlemanly like.

But nothing happened other than him getting in the driver's seat and speeding away.

Nothing happened, that is, until the RPGs exploded from the culvert just outside of town and blew the van off the road and into the frozen empty fields that in the spring would be planted with potatoes. Potatoes for large French fries. Large French fries and frozen hash browns. Hash browns. With ketchup. Ketchup like blood. Like Irene lying dead in a pool of ketchup and the hoard of trenchies coming up quickly on the smashed-up van.

Chapter 5

The ocean. The sound of the ocean. I did not know where the sound was coming from, and I did not know how I could be anywhere near an ocean. The last thing I remembered I had been outside Plummer, Idaho, driving I-don't-know-where with Irene the turncoat trenchie.

Blood. I remember bloody Irene lying on the ground beside a van.

My head hurt. I could not open my eyes at first. I lay in some kind of moist, cushioned soil. Soil. Soil. The echo was getting worse. I lay in some kind of soil and my head hurt and I could hear the ocean.

I wept. That triggered the kind of recollection that you never know if it's a true memory or a mere product of an active and intelligent imagination. I had wept once before when I was this close to a flash.

I sat up suddenly with my eyes wide open, and the daylight overwhelmed the sensors in the back of my eyeballs. The sky was a light gray. Overcast. Overcast. Overcast. It was light gray and overcast, but it was bright compared to the depth of darkness from which I had emerged.

I was in a dense fir forest on a high hill overlooking the ocean.

Something told me I wasn't in Idaho anymore.

The clearing I was in gave a view out to the sea.

The ground around me was covered in fir needles and de-composed plant matter.

Other than the sound of the sea, it was quiet. Quiet. Quiet. (quiet)

How much time had passed since I'd been in Idaho, I had no clue. An hour, a day, a month? I could not tell.

Not another soul was around. Nor another body neither.

The tear dripped down my cheek, and I remembered that I had remembered something that had happened to me another time this close to a flash.

I am never at fault. Now that sounds cocky, but it is true—at least in relation to my job. They don't give me the details of my brief. I get hints and suggestions, but mostly they assign Time Walkers to specific incarnations where their natural character leads them to fulfill whatever brief they need satisfied. That saying you humans have, "Be yourself," is actually a fundamental law for us.

So it's time for me to make a flash. Maybe in the Palouse Range, maybe in the Brooks Range. I get my shit together and do what I can based on what I know. I just act as I see fit, and everything works out. Out. Out. Being myself.

But it isn't working out. I got stuck in a rut. Spinning my wheels. Couldn't get out of Idaho. Trapped in one bar or diner after another. It's what came naturally to me. Hiding from trenchies. Drowning in the bottle to fuck them up. I was being myself, okay? Goddamn it, I was just being my fucking self.

Bitch took off on me. Fuck. That still hurts. The trees, the ocean, the cool, briny breeze could not clear out the memory of that woman driving off in my fucking truck. Let her die. Isn't the first fucking time. Won't be the last. Last. Last. Fuck-ing last.

I lay down again and stared at the gray whiteness through the branches above me.

Same things as last time. I was just being myself, and maybe I fucked up, because when I am incarnated I am just as human as the rest of you...well, mostly. I do get the token bag. And there is z. But I mean my feelings, right? Not just my feelings, but my fallibility too. Fallibility. Fallibility. Fallibility. Fuck up. It's not my fault, but I fuck up.

Those trenchies just flooded the fucking place. As I said it happened before. Once.

Here, it was quiet. No trenchies. No z. No abandoning bitches.

Once before. I remember. I wept.

I mean, they are supposed to put me in the place and time where my natural character will lead me on the right path with the right hints and suggestions. So if I get sucked into a recursive loop, or just go off the deep end for any reason, it reflects on them, right? Reflects on their ability to judge the right assignment for me.

I remember weeping. I remember it was related to a mini-flash. But I can barely remember. I can't remember. I can remember but not remember.

Or it's not on me at all. It's them and the trenchies and something broken in the whole galactic cluster fuck. Someone thought it through enough to mini-flash me out of trouble and onto the right track. Or at least a track that would put me near enough the right track to be right enough.

Mini-flash. Made me weep. If only I could remember. Remember enough. Enough to stop the echo. Echo. Echo.

I like the quiet. Things are always too hectic this close to a release. Release from one incarnation to another. And now all is suspended. I won't even look at the token bag or the GPS. I have no responsibility. They fuck with me, they fuck up. They fuck with my life. They fuck up. What am I supposed to do? Be myself. The first law of Time Walkers. What does my nature lead me to do now? Close off myself from the whole fucking lot of them. Ignore my communications and lie low. From every. last. fucking. being. in. the. infiniteverse.

Another tear.

I stood and looked around. The breeze dried the tear on my cheek, but my eyes watered again and another tear dropped.

I have hidden from them often. They take it into account now, although the first few times they chalked me up to the trenchies. I'm not going anywhere. I just hide out when things get too balled up for one Time Walker to handle.

A pile of boulders a little up the hill beckoned to my den instinct. Behind the boulders was a small cave. If it was small enough, I could create a local Time Closet, and not even Aunt Jenny could find me. But I only had the strength to sustain the closet for an hour or so. But while I'm in it, I have all the time I need to recuperate.

Weeping. What happened before to make me weep? What was the mini-flash? It had been the Port of Amsterdam. Scott Walker, David Bowie, and Jacques Brel were on a bender with me. Keeping the trenchies at bay. The red-light district was impervious to the trenchies. But they had it surrounded. It was a siege, and all I could do was drink and fuck, making no progress toward my flash point.

They had to mini-flash me to Transylvania so I could make my flash in the Carpathian Mountains. I wept for hours when I woke in that damn coffin. But it was nice and isolated. Once it got dark outside, though, the body I shared it with woke up. I got out of there quickly and found my flash point.

I never did know why things had been fucked up that time either. Now I at least have a hint. I had touched the Void. Eloise had entered the Void. She was a lying bitch, though. Fuck her. Fuck her in the most figurative way possible. Possible. Possible. Figurative. How could the Void be so fucking sensitive?

I implemented the Time Closet in the small cloister of boulders.

The Void. Like I would have even known about the Void if they hadn't pointed it out. How many flashes had I made without thinking about looking for such a thing. Then that damn class. The Principles of Manifold Sardonics. I told them it was beyond me. The Principles of Singlefold Sardonics had been more than I needed for my job. For my sense of humor. For my natural level of inertia. Inertia. Inertia. Someone had the bright idea in the name of professional development to try to educate the masses. Didn't work for Northison in 1883, and I didn't believe it would work for them—especially as it applied to me.

I will ask you to get out of my Time Closet. Leave me alone now. I can't hold this Time Closet forever. You are intruding on my precious hour. Hour. Hour.

* * *

The seminar on the Principles of Sardonics took place during a pause between incarnations. The rumor was that Aunt Jenny's bastard cousin had thrown together the class and begged her to allow him to teach it to the rank-and-file. Cover the basics. The concepts. Introduce the talent to the general idea and identify those whom they could recruit into the full course. You had to be certified in the full course to enter The Void on official business, such business being primarily either maintenance of the Manifold or security detail to capture and punish the likes of Eloise who had entered without official clearance and training. A few scientific expeditions set out each season, but those places were reserved for the most pretentious professors who had been published in only the most obscure and pretentious publications.

He was a clown. Professor Rufus T. Eisenstein, PDQ. He was some kind of cross between Groucho Marx and Alexander Nevsky, only with a good deal of superficial knowledge in Sardonics thrown in to boot. I still would lay five-to-two that Nevsky knew more about Sardonics than Rufus T., but even I knew better than to piss off Aunt Jenny and her commitment to nepotism.

I had avoided the class long enough that they had to suspend my Time Walker license until such time as I completed the class. Bureaucracy always gets you in the end, even in my world.

I sat in back and slept through most of it. It was while he was lecturing on the Space-Time-Truth continuum that Rufus T. Eisenstein, PDQ, noticed my lack of commitment to Aunt Jenny's nepotism.

The eraser flew from the front of the lecture hall and caught me square in the forehead. I saw it coming, but I was daydreaming and had neither the will nor the reflexes to catch it. The class laughed. Well, I said the guy was a clown. The junior Time Walkers who were dutifully abiding by orders and taking their dose of Sardonics were delighted with my humiliation. Humiliation is too strong a word. At least compared to what happened next.

"Mitch," Rufus T. enunciated pointedly and exactly, "What is the conceptual toolset used to calculate Truth according to the general theory of Sardonics?"

This would be a good time for z to show up. Nothing.

I thought back to my course in Singlefold Sardonics and delighted the class with my answer. "Propositional First-Order Logic," The giggles and titters gave me goose bumps of shame.

"No!" Rufus T. shouted and slammed his pointer across the lectern. "That's *Special* theory of Sardonics! That only applies to calculating Truth outside the influence of a gravitational field."

Well, it's not like I had been paying attention. Only now everyone knew it. I would have to feign a little interest from here on out to keep the attention off me.

"Eloise Potemkin," Rufus T. said, pointing to the hot chick in the front who had been making eyes with the professor and wearing an all-too-revealing outfit, "Please explain for our village ignoramus the conceptual toolset used to calculate Truth according to the *General* Theory of Sardonics."

The hot chick stood up and turned to the class. She looked nothing like she would so many flashes later when I still would not remember that she was the same bitch who had tried to bury me in that damn class.

"The *General* Theory of Sardonics consists of calculating Truth within a gravitational field using the Eisenstein Field Equations," Eloise began with all the charm of a know-it-all schoolgirl. "The *Special* Theory of Sardonics, and its reliance on Propositional First-Order Logic, can only give a reliable result in a single point in the five-and-a-half dimensions of Space-Time-Truth. This is called Instantaneous Truth."

Rufus T. had had enough. "That's good Ms. Potemkin, now—"

Eloise Potemkin had not had enough. "But the entire surface and volume of Truth in a gravitational Manifold can be calculated with the Eisenstein Field Equations, including each individual point. Thus, the *General* Theory of Sardonics completely supersedes the *Special* Theory of Sardonics."

"That's enough, Ms. Pot—"

Eloise had still not had enough. She unbuttoned yet another button of her blouse. "Furthermore, the *Special* Theory of Sardonics only vaguely suggests, infers, and implies the equivalence principle between The Absolute and The Relative, while the Eisenstein Field Equations derive Hodge's Constant according to the processes of third-order differential trigonometry. Hodge's Constant establishes the equivalence between The Absolute and The Relative in the one-and-a-half dimensions of Truth that exist above the three dimensions of space and the single dimension of time."

By now, Rufus T. was as entranced with the blouse as much as the rest of the class was.

Eloise persisted, "The Eisenstein Field Equations supersede Hodge's Law, but only in the compound dimensions of both Truth and Half-Truth. For Time Walkers on the planet earth, the dimension of Half-Truth is enough, and this is approximated closely enough by the *Special* Theory of Sardonics and its complementary tools of Propositional First-Order Logic. Few humans even bother with The Truth, whether in a gravitational Manifold or the highly theoretical Singlefold Containium. If all you're going to do is spend your time wandering the earth like Kwai Chang Caine or David Banner, then you're just wasting your time with this theory shit."

Rufus T. took his eyes off her Double-T Truths. I could see that he was aware that her words were diverging from the point and would touch on dangerous ground if he didn't take back control—but damn, those Double-T Truths of hers were something even he couldn't ignore!

"But if you have any interest in entering The Void—" Eloise said, putting special emphasis on The Void. The rest of the class forgot about her Double-T Truths and looked at each other as though just introduced to the most life-changing concept of all time (which they had been). I stared at Eloise. Eloise and Rufus T. His concentration on her cleavage broke and his consternation with her words rose.

Eloise blurted out the warning before Rufus T. could stop her, "If you have any interest in entering The Void, " she repeated, "You better be on top of your calculations. The truth dilation that occurs at the inflection points of the Manifold under gravitational stress can crack the whole thing from stem to stern, and you and the rest of the infiniteverse can crack with it if you haven't calculated the Sardonic Truth to the nth degree."

Eloise sat down before Eisenstein erupted. "That is highly irregular and equally irresponsible to discuss such matters in this seminar," he shouted. "Everyone, forget what you have heard! The Void is a concept that can only be understood after a complete immersion in the mysteries of the relativity of absolute simultaneity."

Eloise smirked at the rest of the class.

Bitch.

Rufus T. Eisenstein rushed through the rest of the lecture and did not wake me from my slumber again—even when he elucidated his precious Eisenstein Field Equations. At the next break, he re-issued my license and told me he wanted me out of his fucking class. I obliged in no time.

But no one, not even me, could forget something as awesome as the concept of The Void. Once spoken, it could not be unspoken. Not even by Aunt Jenny, although she did eliminate Rufus T.'s class once and for all and sent him to tend her begonias on the far side of The Void.

* * *

Something was wrong. I could only sustain the Time Closet for forty-five minutes. I'm always good for an hour, but that time, forty-five was it.

I walked to the other side of the hill and found an old logging road. It was time to head back to the fray before they got too worried about me. Even Achilles had taken some time out from battle to pout.

I had not been walking long when a beat-up old pickup truck clattered down the road. The fat driver with a stubbled auburn beard offered me a ride. Said he was a logger fresh off clearing another clear-cut. His third that week.

His passenger looked as though one more wit would have made him a half-wit.

It didn't look like there was much room in the cab, so I jumped in the bed and slapped the roof with my palm.

"No, no, sunshine," the driver said, sticking his ratty head out the window, "Let Cooter ride in back."

The scrawny kid from the passenger seat, presumably Cooter, popped out of the truck and into the bed.

"Shit," I said when I had slammed the door. "You got the nerve, z."

"Like my outfit?" z said, jamming the gearshift into first.

"What's with Cooter?"

z just giggled.

"Play time is over, snugglebuns," z said.

"Don't wink at me like that, z. How did I end up here?"

z doffed his oily baseball cap and slicked back his slimy hair and popped the cap back on again. I'd never seen z in such an outrageous uniform. Outrageous, yes, but not so...dirty!

"The Manifold is breaking loose. The trenchies are flooding the main flash zones. You came across a deviant trenchie—Irene, the trenchie bleeding beside the van—and we had to flash you out of there before the trenchie internal affairs platoon caught up with and finished off that poor sod."

I let the road bounce past us for some time.

"What's my brief now?"

z fingered the steering wheel like it was a Steinway. "Same as before. Your first flash point is your only."

"But I'm even further away now than before. Are the trenchies leaving the Palouse?"

"They're flooding in even more desperately."

"You sure I'm not supposed to go to the Brooks Range?" I watched z for any kind of exceptional reaction. Well, exceptional for z anyway.

"First flash point is the only, buttercup."

I knew better than to ask how. I knew z wanted me to ask, but I also knew I would only get the standard, "Be yourself, Mitch," so I kept my mouth shut just because I knew he wanted me to ask.

We drove on in silence. At the bottom of the hill, we turned onto a highway.

"Where are we, anyway?"

"Just a jouncy and a bop from Depoe Bay, Oregon. Cooter's brother runs a fishing smack out of the harbor there. Will get you up the coast to Astoria. Up to you to find your way to Portland from there."

z hummed *Great Balls of Fire*.

"What's in fucking Portland?"

"Don't swear around me, motherfucker," z said, then z had a short fit of hysteria. z reached out the driver side window and Cooter touched z's hand. The hysteria dissipated.

"Instructions will arrive in Portland. Everyone's playing it all by ear now. Heard a rumor Portland Petroleum runs a bi-weekly flight to Point Barrow, Alaska. We're working to get you on board."

"So the Brooks Range it is?"

z turned to me in a fury. A furry fury. "Mitch, I told you thirteen times and I'll tell you another thirteen, your only flash point remains your primary flash point. And I also told you the entire organization, even beyond Aunt Jenny, is play-ing everything by ear, so be a good boy and do likewise, will you now?"

I shrugged. Something wasn't adding up. Eloise crept back into my consciousness. The bitch from Moscow, not the bitch from Principles of Sardonics, even if they always had been one and the same. Damn bitch. Damn me for...nevermind.

We pulled into the marina. Cooter wanted to help with my luggage. I told him I traveled luggage-free.

z led me to a dilapidated fishing smack. "Mind the gap," z said as we stepped from the dock onto the deck.

"Permission to come aboard?" z called out in a high-pitched prissy voice.

"z," I said, quietly, "don't you notice the color of the boat?"

"Yellow ochre is an appropriate camouflage, eh?" z replied. "And if nothing else her name should put your mind at ease."

I checked the bow and found the following word emblazoned in Marine Corps pink: "Potemkin"

Eloise. Bitch was still haunting me.

"Reassuring, that," I said.

"Hey, I'm the only prig here allowed to speak in uptight Angloese," z said.

With a giggle and a grunt, Cooter's brother Sigmund stepped out of the galley and onto the deck.

Chapter 6

"Got news for you," Sigmund said leaning on the *Potemkin's* wheel. "Foul weather and a heavy thick fog. The approaches to Astoria are closed."

A late December afternoon was upon us. The flat gray daylight was going fast. I stood with Sigmund in the *Potemkin's* wheelhouse. The ship heaved to and fro, up and down in the heavy seas. Waves crashed over the bow and, as the water washed over the window, my view was for a moment obscured. Not that it made a whole hell of a lot of difference.

"Foul weather," I said. "Fucking fantastic."

I never caught Sigmund's last name. Don't even know if he had one. Didn't really matter either way.

It'd been only a mere four hours earlier that we'd cast off from Depoe Bay.

"Best be getting underway," Sigmund had said to *z* and me as we stood on the deck, all the while minding the gap. "A foul wind out of the north is picking up. Best we be out of port."

z had delivered a mock salute. "Aye, Captain."

"Asshole. You go get with Cooter," Sigmund had said. "We cast off in five minutes."

z had blown him a kiss. "Love you too, Sigmund. Ah, I love the open sea! Makes you a real man. Lucky you, Mitch. Lucky you. I, however, will not be partaking in this sea adventure."

I'd been ignoring z. For as outlandish as he is, I seldom paid him much mind. Like most humans and their bosses.

z had pulled my attention back after muttering something about a complete and utter fuckin' dissolution of the Manifold.

z had adjusted his worn jeans, making his bulbous gut even more pronounced. "They've found a crack. A new way in. The Manifold is dying. Here. You'll need this."

z had presented me the butt of a pistol. "Take it, Mitch."

"I've got my own resources."

z had laughed. "You never were any good at poker. You could never hold 'em. Playing crap and praying for luck on the river. A pair of jacks always tripped you up because they never trip! I believe you'll find that little bag of tricks of yours is out of reach. Out of time, as it were. Don't look so surprised. You can't bluff, either. Not like Ivey."

I had tried for the token bag. No response.

"It's simple, really," z had said. "You can't fold Truth-Time anymore. You see, Mitch? It's the end of the world. Doom and gloom and all that. You liked going native. You've done it before. Now, you have nothing to get by on but your bravado. No cheating with the bag anymore. Be yourself. Remember the credo! Take the pistol. Now."

I had reached out and taken the Glock. "Got any cash? I only have fifty bucks and change."

z nodded his head and reached into his pocket of his sullied jeans. "Dear, oh, dear. Poor Mitch. I've got a twenty. You owe me. Again. The bottle of bourbon is mine, though. Keep your fuckin' hands off of it. I'll need it to help me drive home. Portland, Mitch. Portland. In two days, meet Monique on the steps of the Portland Art Museum at high noon. It's time you grow up and decide what's important. Put up or shut up, as the natives are fond of saying."

The blast of the *Potemkin's* twin diesels turning over had put an end to our conversation.

And, now, back in the *Potemkin's* wheelhouse I stood with Sigmund. The waves were high as he took the bow into a trough. The sun was dying.

Sigmund always, always had a hand-rolled little cigar hanging out the side of his mouth. The wheelhouse reeked of the shit—so much so that I'd asked him for one to join in the fun.

"These are special cigars," Sigmund said. "Powerful. Most powerful. Get the leaves from a special shop south of Portland. Sal and something it be called."

"Is it just me, or are you sounding more and more like a pirate with each paragraph?" I said.

"Arrgghh," Sigmund said.

I took the slim cigar and lit up.

By the second puff, I no longer gave a shit about the heaving boat or the storm. By the second cigar, I was laughing nonstop as old "Salty" Sigmund recalled tales of sexual adventure and admonishment during his stint in the Merchant Marines.

"Potemkin. Interesting name," I said.

Sigmund told me to fuck off, and then he said it had something to do with his ex wife.

"Her name was Potemkin?"

"No!" Sigmund yelled over the wash of the waves. "You idiot. I bet you wait for the river with nothing but a pair of jacks. Her name was Eriss. A woman who liked discord, that's for goddamn sure! Enjoyed it. Got real pissed if she wasn't invited to parties. She had a thing for the Greeks. I could stand this. I like Greeks too, if you understand my meaning. Not in a mano-a-mano way, either. She left me for a foreign exchange student. Really! She did! Varguennes. A Frog from Nice who was finishing his graduate degree in the poetry of

France. He was a French Navy lieutenant! She would pine for him out on the dock. Like she was something out of a novel."

A beat.

"Eriss," he started again as another wave crashed over the bow. "I hauled apples because of her. Always had a favorite. Golden Delectable. That was her brand."

He pulled a golden apple from the crate next to the wheel. "Nothing but the finest apples fresh from the warehouse. I used to run non-Washington apples into Seattle! Dangerous work. Paid well."

An indistinguishable squawk from the radio.

"Coast Guard. Said it's too dangerous on the Bar," Sigmund said. "We best wait for daylight to try that run. Go below and tell one of my crew to bring me a hot meal and my bottle. I'll be here for the duration. Or until we sink. We're at anchorage. Tell 'em I'll be dropping the sea anchor."

"Crew?" I said.

"My wife and my two daughters," Sigmund said. A glint in his eyes in the evaporating light of the day. "You best get below, son. Beware though! Show them that apple of yours at your own risk! Choose well. Choose wisely. There's no coming back from the Void once the die is cast."

I pocketed the apple and swung open the wheelhouse door at the same time a wave crashed over me.

"Shut the goddamn hatch!" Sigmund said.

It was cold. I hate the cold. Now my sweater was soaked. I slipped down the bridge ladder to the unstable deck, which continued to move under my feet like a carousel on meth. A heave starboard. I was flung against the interior plank wall of the ship. I bashed my head pretty well and felt the run of warm blood down the left side of my face.

As I lay on my back on the deck, three young women emerged from the hold: a blond with long flowing hair, a brunette, and a red head, her hair cropped and spiky.

"Is he dead?" the blond said.

"No," the red head said. "He's a pussy. I told Papa we shouldn't have taken him on."

"Let's get him below," the brunette said.

The three of them drug me down into the darkness of the hold. I arrived in a narrow long berth that ran the length of the *Potemkin*. In the dim auburn light, I could just make out the three women in identical gray jumpsuits looking at me and discussing something among themselves.

The ship heaved. The Golden Delectable slid out of my pocket and rolled across the deck. I grabbed it before it'd strayed too far.

"An apple!" the blond said. "Give it to me!"

The brunette moved between the blond and me. "Easy, Aphrodite. He's got to choose."

"You do spoil things, Hera," Aphrodite said. "I saw it first."

The redhead lit a cigar and took a swig from a bourbon bottle. "Both of you shut up. It's mine. The spoils of war and all that."

Hera pulled her long dark hair away from her face. "Don't upset the apple cart, Athena."

All three of them glared at me. "Who gets it, Mitch?"

I drifted to apathy. The rocking of the ship lulling me into the oblivion. "Why do I need to choose? Your father has a whole crate of them."

"It's not that simple, Mitch," Hera said. "We don't like it anymore than you, but the die's been cast. By you! You must choose one of us."

"Which one of us do you like best, Mitch?" Aphrodite said. "That's who the apple should go to. Do you know Paris?"

"I don't like Paris," I said. "The city stinks of the French and their poetry."

"Just like Papa," Athena said. "He might be redeemable after all."

"It's time to shower, ladies!" Aphrodite announced. "He can judge after that."

"Shit!" Hera shook her head and spoke to Athena. "A dirty old man came up with this contest. Your Papa always refuses my request to bring the rules up-to-date. Yet he lets you make *just war* with whomever the hell you want. Go figure."

I lit up another of the Sigmund's special cigars. Time was immobile. I was immobile. Well, most of me was anyway as the three women continued to slip out of their clothes. In slow motion, no less.

All three were now nude, although Athena had refused to remove the sheathed diving knife strapped to her lower leg.

Finally! Bodies!

Each of them sported a lotus flower tattoo on her left hip. The hot steamy water flowed over their supple skin. I cursed that procedure that took the adjectival namesake of Brazil and involved paraffin. It cheated a man. Looking at the three women, I couldn't ascertain what was real and what was L'Oreal. Damn!

The women bathed in the open shower tossing a loofa around. The loofa, ship-like, struggled as it navigated over the heaving swell of hips and breasts, hugged the curves and the long bare legs, making its way to Heaven.

To Nirvana.

The wave of apathy continued its slow roll over me. Portland was my destination. I should be striving to get there. I should be up in the wheelhouse with Sigmund helping him get through this storm. Problem was, I didn't give a shit and was watching three incredibly hot women frolicking in the shower. The world had stopped. This world. It was hazy below deck. I couldn't move.

Hera's body glistened in the dim light. "Mitch. If you choose me, I'll make you a captain. The master of all you see. Give you a new life away from your troubles. You do have troubles, Mitch. They haunt you. I'll get you your own ship. Give you Papa's ship. Leave your other life behind. Be here with me. Stop running from your demons."

"Don't listen to Hera," Athena said, bourbon bottle still in hand even as she showered. "I could give you knowledge so powerful you wouldn't have those longing questions anymore. You could end your quest. You have been doubting lately, Mitch. Don't you want it all to just stop? To know the answer? To know why you're here? I'd also give you the skills to win a really nasty bar fight."

Aphrodite was silent. She turned her long thin-waisted back to me and ran her fingers through her wet flowing teased blond hair then across the lotus tattoo on the curve of her hip.

"I'll make her yours," Aphrodite said, her voice low and quiet. "Your woman. The one who left you behind. Left you alone, by yourself, to deal with all this. All alone. You're lonely, Mitch. That I do know. She's there for the asking. Come on, Mitch. You know you want it. Want her. She's waiting for you out there. Choose me. Choose her."

This was tough. Tested me. Their offers. Their oh-so-inviting nubile bodies.

Could make her yours.

Enough of that. She'd been the one who'd left me in Idaho. She'd made her goddamn choice. It was my time to choose.

The three of them were like goddesses in the water. Or, perhaps it was the smoke. Or the heaving of the ship. Or my apathy.

I lit up yet another cigar.

The water of the shower stopped. The creaking of the ship filled the Void. Wrapped in towels, the three of them moved in front of me in the steam of the shower and the smoke from my cigar.

Athena finally barked out, "You must choose, Mitch. That's the way it's done."

"Who is it?" Hera said.

Who indeed.

I held the apple in front of me. This was it. My fate, undecided, yet in plain sight right in front of me. The choice of one of the three. It's not like my decision would result in war or anything that dramatic. Well, in theory anyway.

"Aphrodite," I muttered.

"Goddamnit!" Hera said. "It's always her. Must be the mystery of the blond!"

"Typical," Athena said as she threw the empty bourbon bottle at me.

I deeply inhaled the cigar's foul smoke. Shit, I wish I could choose all three of them!

Aphrodite let the towel slip off of her body, the lotus flower tattoo on her hip glimmering. She was warm and moist from the shower.

I held out the apple.

She took it.

She moved over me as Hera and Athena dissolved in the fog of the smoke.

"You won't be sorry, Mitch," she said. "Come here. Time to storm the walls of Troy."

* * *

Goddamn token bag!

I don't remember how many jumps have gone by since I'd first learned to use the token bag. To fold reality and make the opening. More than a hundred jumps? A thousand? An eternity? But, eternity is not forever. Just a really long time.

He had shown me the secret in the Wasteland. After I'd done my penance in the Time Closet.

Spirits when they please
Can either sex assume, or both.

Among other things.

He had been in the Wasteland. Had showed me how to fold reality. Had told me the truth about the Void. Not Aunt Jenny's Truth or that Sardonics shit.

It had been John. The same John I'd help put in the ground so many days ago in Boise.

That John.

"Be yourself," he had said.

At first, I didn't know I was in the Wasteland. I'd made what I thought had been a clean Assumption.

I'd not met the outbound Time Walker, not that that was unusual, but there were also no remnants. I hadn't assumed a dead man. I awoke lying on the ground.

I stood up. My body was not heavy. Not burdened. I had a long gritty knife strapped to my waist with a wide leather belt and was dressed in sandals and a long robe. I was covered in the red dust that seemed to be all around me for as far as I could see.

Overhead a heavy red bloated sun pressed over the plain.

I'd awoken in the Wasteland. An alternate. I'd jumped well past my initial target. Time was out of sorts here. Stillness, stillness, and none to think, kind of like water on a boat that sinks.

The rough of that red-rust broad naked plain I was on spread in all directions and was lifeless except for the scattered waist-high purple of the sage plants. But a verdant valley lay off in the distance, and I set off for it.

Of Mans First Disobedience, and the Fruit
Of that Forbidden Tree, whose mortal taste
Brought Death into the World, and all our woe,
With loss of Eden, till one greater Man
Restore us, and regain the blissful Seat,

I was supposed to be in Kansas. That much I had known pre-jump. But, no remnants. No images. A blank. I didn't know who I was. What I was.

The Valley beckoned as I neared. I saw no animals let alone another form like mine. I knew one thing for sure: I wasn't in Kansas. A moment went past me, whisked away on the wind.

I stopped at the bank of the wide river that separated me from the entrance to the Valley. A rickety wooden boat was moored in still water.

And Utnapishtim looking at him from the distance
Began thinking within himself, and
With himself he thus meditated:
"Why are ['those with stones'] of the ship smashed?
*And one, who has not my * * * rides in [the ship].*
He that comes there [is he?] not a man, and has he not
the 'right side' of a man?
*I look: (Is that) * * * not [a human being?]*
*I look: (Is that) * * * not [a man?]*
*I look: (Is that) * * * [not a god?]*
He resembles me in every respect."

I climbed down the ravine. I stopped on and off to get the grit out of my sandals. I pushed off in the boat, and I made my way across the dark water to the Otherside.

On the far side, I left the boat on the bank, and I climbed up the ravine.

Filling the Void

The oasis was below me. A pool of black water bordered by a strip of green lushness running across the Wasteland. I entered the Valley garden and drank from the pool. I had no reflection in the pool no matter how hard I tried to find one. I was definitely a man—that much I'd known since my Assumption. Kind of hard to let that escape your notice.

I unbelted my sheathed knife and took off my dusty robe and slipped into the pool. The rejuvenation. The rebirth.

> *And Gilgamesh saw a pool wherein was cool (and re-*
> *freshing) water;*
> *He stepped into it and poured out some water.*
> *A (demon in the shape of a) serpent darted out; the*
> *plant slipped [away from his hands];*
> *he came [out of the pool?], and took the plant away,*
> *and as he turned back, he uttered a curse (?).*
> *And after this Gilgamesh sat down and wept.*

Time passed. I climbed out of the pool. A sudden warm breeze blew in and dried my body in the deep red setting sun. It was still. It was quiet.

Nude, I lay down on a run of soft green grass that ran from the water's edge up to the bank of a small cliff a ways behind me. I closed my eyes and slept. Time went by, but yet didn't. The sun faded. I opened my eyes.

A crack of branches. Someone else was in paradise. Someone at the edge of the pool.

With a sudden jolt, I sat up and unsheathed my knife.

I looked.

He stood at the edge of the pool a short distance from me. He also had no reflection in the black water of the pool. His robe was like mine, the hood over his head, his body fit. He wasn't surprised to see me.

"You look hungry," he said. "Take an apple."

The late-afternoon setting red sun broke through the thick conifers climbing up either side of the valley.

I jumped up and held the knife in front of me. "I do know how to use this."

He neared. A single drop of blood dripped from his hand into the cold water, dissolving and making its way deep down in the pool.

The hood of his robe obscured most of his face.

"You never did sound that tough, Mitch."

I dropped the knife.

He lifted his hood.

John.

Afterwards, we sat nude on the grass. His back was to me. He was bald.

"The Truth is malleable," John said. "That's its core strength. You can mold it to whatever outcome you need. This becomes the Truth. The old was the Before Truth. Bruth. Histrionics concerns itself with the transition between the two Truth States."

"That's not what they taught us," I said.

"Do you know why you're here, Mitch? In this place? With me? Here and now."

Even z wouldn't have been able to provide me with a satisfactory explanation of that. Eloise. Perhaps Eloise.

"'Here and now.'" I said. "You sound like a poet."

He stood up. "Time doesn't matter here. Doesn't exist, actually. Not time like they know it." He paused, then continued with vigor, "The Void is a conduit, Mitch! A passage through Truth-Time that connects the Absolute Truth with reality. Their reality. That's why the Prime Movers keep it closed down. That's why it's forbidden."

"I don't bother with the Void. I know the protocol. The boundaries of my brief."

"There's a war on, Mitch," John said. "The game is afoot. It's not good versus evil. Those are antiquated terms for something they can barely grasp. An idea omnipresent, but still out of reach. Some humans see it and are driven mad by it. The indirects. They've been touched."

"You're talking nonsense, John."

John said, "You can enter the Void with the Knowledge! My knowledge. If you enter without it, you'll upset the Balance. The Void dissolves. The gateway closes. Until the Gathering. Until the Prime Movers create the infiniteverse Manifold again."

"And, this is why all hell is breaking loose. Right..."

"It's not child's play, Mitch. Once upon a time, you missed your flash point. Left me to die. That was the key! Don't you understand? I missed my final flash point! I'm one of them now."

"You can't miss the final flash point," I said. "There's nothing. It's the end."

"You're wrong," John said. "You made me, Mitch. Don't you understand? I shouldn't have died back there. You shouldn't have been at my funeral. You were supposed to make the Assumption for me. But you didn't and that's when I drifted into the Void. I can show you a method. Teach you. Give you something of me to take with you. Show you how to access it. You'll be accessing me. When you need it. A space in Truth-Time to hold tokens. Things you might need. That's my gift to you. But, I must have a token from you."

He extracted my blade and cut himself down his palm. "What is a token but a fixture in a certain place and time? A device you use to recreate what was in the here and now? I'm out of time, Mitch. So are you."

"What are you? My keeper?" I said.

He handed me the blade.

"You're out of time, Mitch. Even in a place such as this. You must be gone before the night runs its course," John stood up and held out his bloody palm. "Cast the die. Set things into motion. Touch the Void."

I left him before dawn and made the ridge by sunrise. In the red of the dust, I could make the burned out valley of the *locus amoenus* below me.

Blood oath. My hand still burned with the scar. I'd lived a lie for so very long, it was hard to stop it now.

I continued my climb up the ridge and out of the valley. The dust storm picked up and the forest smelled dead, the trees stripped of their leaves and the mess of it slick under my sandals.

Farewell happy fields,
Where joy forever dwells: Hail, horrors, hail.

I stood on the ridge. A white flash filled the emptiness and overran me, surged through my form.

I flashed. I jumped. Assumption. Then, the pain. I had been hurt, maybe even dead for an instance in time.

My shoulder and left arm.

I folded Truth-Time and made the cut in the continuum for the first time. Summoned the token bag and extracted the healing device. I placed the device on my chest and let it do its work as I drifted in and out of this Truth-Time reference of my incarnation.

I was on the ground. In the dust of Kansas. The high noon sun directly overhead, the heat from it pouring down over me.

Blood was everywhere, both blood from me and the corpse of a man just a few meters from me, his head had been smashed in by the blood soaked rock next to my hand. I'd been in a fight. Or so it appeared.

I wrapped my bleeding arm in his shirt. I was next to a set of rail tracks. A hand car was nearby. I field stripped the corpse for whatever it could offer me, which wasn't much. A long knife, some coins, and a rifle of some sort. And a hand-written note. I was back in time. Back to yet another brief.

I was in Kansas. z would have said this was a mis-jump. Shit happens.

I read the note with John Brown's name scrawled on it. Kansas. Bleeding Kansas. For a short period of time, anyway.

* * *

I opened my eyes to the morning late-fall peeling sun. The Winter Solstice beckoned.

Yellow ochre sky in morning, Time Walker take warning.

I stood on the docks of Astoria. Near Ithaca Road. The moorings were empty. The *Potemkin* gone in the fog.

I reached up to the sore on my head. The crusted blood from last night.

I extracted the business card from my pocket.

Troy Marlow's

Columbia River Boat Tours

See the sites of Portland from the water!
Leaving Astoria daily

Seventy bucks and change in my pocket, and a Glock tucked down the back of my pants.

Portland by high noon tomorrow.

I hoped Captain Marlow wouldn't need a credit card.

Chapter 7

I'll probably never learn. It's the kind of remorse one only contemplates when the shit has hit the fan and you're the only one around to clean it up. Or more specifically, when you crawl out of the freezing Columbia River, naked and alone, counting as your only blessing that you are still around to count blessings—and then it begins to snow.

Marlow had proven to be a trenchie. I had missed all the signs, but then the signs had not appeared as I have been conditioned to recognize them.

No yellow ochre trench coat. No yellow ochre anything— at least what I could see. Maybe yellow ochre underwear, just for a gag. No dead-eyed gaze as though they are looking ten feet behind you. Troy Marlow had looked me square in the eyes and taken my seventy bucks for the trip up river, even smiling when he shrugged off the five bucks I was short of his posted fare.

Had those been yellow ochre stains on his rotting teeth?

I climbed up the embankment, grasping at fern fronds and rotting limbs of decaying logs. The damp, mossy soil smelled of compost, and it reminded me of the time I tended earthworms for Darwin. What a scamp, he.

The slope was steep, and the hill high. It rose abruptly from the river and extended into the clouds. No telling how far I would have to climb before I got to a clearing that would show me some sign of civilization. A road. A house. A man. A woman. A woman. A woman. A damn bitch who leaves you at the first sign of trouble. Aphrodite had promised, but I never put much stock in such clever games anyway. Worst-case scenario had been getting a night in the hold with her as we stormed the walls of Troy.

The snow wasn't sticking to the ground, but it pricked my bare back and shoulders. It melted on contact with my skin and trickled in frigid streams down my sides, down my ass, down my legs.

At forty-five (in human years), I find my faculties becoming blunt. Maybe that accounts for my miss on Marlow. But I also find myself fortified and toughened by those twenty-five years of experience—even in such an ephemeral time as the twenty-first century. A man is a man after all, and when you have a job to do, you do it, even after swimming half a wide winter river in the snow.

At noon the following day, I was to be in Portland. That was my job. Those words were all I had left to go on. *Portland, tomorrow at noon. Monique.* It was the only tool I had, the only weapon I had to fend off the elements and circumstance. An idea. Go ahead and strip a man, a Time Walker, a Time Walker as a man, down to nothing. Take away his token bag, remove all contact with both the external and internal worlds, and yet an idea, even an idea as simple as having to be at some specific place at some specific time, is enough to overcome even the most dire of situations. That had gotten us across the desert to Aqaba. That had preserved us on Elephant Island. That's how I had remained married to Cleopatra for a quarter-century. You thought Eloise was a wench. Brother, let me tell you a thing or two.

Portland, tomorrow at noon. Monique. All the way up the hillside. In the snow. Just a man and his dick.

I can't even remember the moment I realized Marlow was a trenchie. What had it been—an hour outside Astoria? I had snoozed. Mind you, I had been up all night with Aphrodite in the hull of that boat. *The* Potemkin, *goddamn it*! When you get the likes of Aphrodite, even in the human world, you take her for all she's worth. And then you take her for more than she's worth so she'll always remember you were the kind of man who not only went all the way, but went beyond all the way and would always go beyond anything she would ever imagine as approximating all the way.

And yet wasn't it someone else I had thought about all the while?

Was I sleeping, or merely ruminating on the relative merits of a goddess and her empty promise versus a bitch and her treachery? In either case, clarity returned when I noticed Troy had the Glock that *z* had given me. I noticed it because he was pointing the barrel in my face.

"We need you," Troy said.

"Who's 'we'?" The only other occupant of Troy Marlow's tour boat was his mongrel dog, Kurtz.

"You know who *we* are, Mitch."

No, I didn't know who *we* were, but I went with it.

"You know I don't have any cash on me," I said.

"The token bag. Give me your token bag." The dog sniffed around my feet. I tried to kick it, but my feet were bound together.

"How'd that happen? When'd you tie me up?"

Troy Marlow spit tobacco juice when he said, "I never knew a man to sleep so deeply."

"You around many men when they sleep?"

The butt of the Glock did not feel too good when he smacked it sharply against the side of my head.

"The fucking token bag, Time Walker!"

"It's broken."

"Bullshit," Troy said as he chambered a round in the Glock.

"Careful with that, I thought you said you needed me."

Troy looked at the gun and then at me.

"Why you act so cavalier?" he asked.

"Ever heard of French poetry?" I parried.

Troy was confused. I saw that telltale dead-eyed gaze and had begun to suspect he was a trenchie. Trenchies don't do well with non-sequiturs. In fact, they don't even do well with any kind of sequitur, non or not non.

"Prudhomme, Boileau-Despreaux..."

"Enough!"

I wouldn't tell him that my cavalier attitude was not merely due to my finely honed sangfroid, but had more to do with my confidence that any pistol given to me by *z*, particularly in most extreme circumstance, was likely to be unloaded. He liked his guns unloaded. Or if it was loaded (to give the proper weight) it was missing its firing pin, or the safety was stuck on.

"Pelletier du Mans..." I continued.

"You will make me do something I will regret!" Troy said.

"My personal favorite, Eustache Deschamps—"

Troy pulled the trigger, but nothing happened.

I sneered.

Troy lowered the Glock and let off the safety.

Bang! The shot rang out. A horrifying howl rose in the cold, gray afternoon air—even more horrifying than anything Alan Ginsberg could produce. Troy had shot his mongrel Kurtz in the hindquarters.

* * *

"No one knows what darkness lurks within the heart of a dog," I said.

Conrad and Bulgakov sat with me smoking African cigars in the hold of another boat in another place and another time. The other boat was the *Roi de Belges*. The other place was another river on another continent. The other time was just before dinner.

Conrad looked at me. "I could use that."

Bulgakov looked at Conrad. "What part? I was thinking I could use that too."

"Joe, Mike, why don't each of you take a piece. There's enough to go round," I said.

Captain Marlowe rang the bell outside the galley. His cook, Margarita, had finished preparing the lobster bisque.

"Finally! Food!" Joe said.

We rushed to the galley and sat humbly while Margarita said a prayer and crossed herself.

"You'd think she'd do that before she cooked, not after!" Mike said.

"Sit down and eat," Captain Chris said imperiously.

"What does it mean to say something 'imperiously'," Margarita asked innocently.

"Go, strumpet! Go and read thine own dictionary," Captain Chris said.

Joe, Mike, and I were too busy eating to take part in this petty domestic drama.

"But, Sir Christopher, you said you would see to my education personally."

The captain squinted at her and glanced at each of us passengers in turn, gauging our approval or disapproval, whichever the case might be. Apparently he thought better than to dismiss her out of hand.

"This is the age of empires. Imperialism is the religion of the land. To be imperious is to act and speak in accordance with the aims and spirit of the empire that you serve! To fail to act or speak imperiously is utter blasphemy!"

"Oh, Captain Marlowe, I am doomed to hell!"

"Now, now, my dear Margarita. Why do you speak thusly?"

"When I asked thee about what it means to say something 'imperiously,' I said it innocently!"

We all laughed. Margarita was embarrassed.

"But why do you all laugh in the face of my doom?"

"Captain Marlowe is full of shit, that's why," Joe said, "Notice how he spells his name with that pretentious English 'e' thrown in at the end? Why, if I were ever to draw upon such a name, the 'e' is the first thing to go. That's the definition of 'imperious' for you."

"You mean 'imperious' means to put the letter 'e' at the end of your name?"

Mike broke in, "If you want it to mean that, toots."

"Then call me Margaritae."

Captain Marlowe was pleased. He knew that her taking his side in public meant he would get some that night. His imperiousness asserted itself.

"Have I told you boys about the adventures of Edward the Second?"

"That was last night's dinner talk," Joe said.

"Dido? I had a hell of a time in Carthage."

"The night before," Mike said.

"This dude I knew in Malta, then?"

"Breakfast two days ago, dear," Margaritae said. She had her hand on the captain's shoulder. She was getting much too carried away with the easy-going feelings. The captain flung her hand away and shot her daggers from his eyes. Just because she would put out didn't mean he had to be wrapped entirely around her finger. He still had to keep up the pretense of 'imperiousness' after all.

"Yes, Master," Margaritae said as she hurried off to the gallery's scullery and ate her gruel while cleaning up the dinner dishes.

"How about The Massacre of Paris?" the Captain asked.

We all three looked at the Captain with eager anticipation. Dribbles of bisque dotted our chins. That was a new story.

The bread was hard, flat bread that made perfect spoons for eating the soup.

Joe slurped his soup and said, "I'd like to hear about the destruction of so fine a city!" and he giggled.

At first I had thought z was Mike, but then I began to suspect that he might have switched things up and was playing Joe—at least for the moment.

"City?" Captain Chris roared. "Who said anything about a city?" And he proceeded to tell us as fine a tale as any we had heard on our whole trip up the dark river.

After the tale was told, Joe and Mike said they would leave the rendering of that one to me. I said I was up to it. And I was.

The next day we arrived at the encampment. The lunatic had left hats impaled on the key posts of the ramparts.

"What they've done to those hats!" Mike squealed. That's settled. Mike was z after all.

"And how did we get here without any attack from the natives?" Joe asked. "What kind of drama is that without racially charged bigoted depictions of backward peoples?"

Mike looked all around, getting a feel for what would be his home for the next six months. He was nonplussed. "And where's the fruity Russian I was promised would be here to greet us?"

O, z, where art thou now?

"Whiners all, you landlubbers," Captain Kit said, throwing the luggage from the *Roi de Belges*'s hold. "Time to settle the bill."

The travel agents in Brazzaville had cautioned us that the captain could be quite ornery about the bill and that we should show a good amount of flexibility in the negotiation.

Judging by the frequent and regular sounds emanating from the captain's state room that kept us awake all the previous night long, he was full of manly humor of which we took heed. We settled the bill at full price. But we speculated among ourselves what would happen if he were to meet the wrong man at the wrong place to settle the wrong bill.

The captain drifted down the river, his arm draped over Margaritae's shoulder and his gun at full attention. "I'll be back in six months," he hollered.

Margaritae called out, "Remember, when it comes to vegetables in the jungle, there's no second freshness. Only first freshness!"

Joe looked at me. "What does she mean by that, Mitch?"

Mike looked at both of us with a twinkle in his eye, "What the devil—I can use that!"

* * *

Troy dropped the Glock and it fired another round. This one also into his dog's hindquarter.

"Kurtz!"

Troy picked up the Glock and threw it over the side of the boat.

There goes that.

"You trenchies end up being all alike, don't you?" I said.

"Why wouldn't we be?" Troy retorted, and of course he was right. "Help me with my dog," he demanded.

"You'll have to untie me," I said.

Troy was distraught, and he wasn't paying much attention to my point of view. He untied me unquestioningly as soon as I mentioned it.

Needless to say, I overpowered the captain immediately and prepared to take myself up river on my own.

I tied up Troy and looked at the howling mongrel.

"At least help the dog, Mitch!"

"You threw away the gun, ochre man!"

"I don't mean kill him. I mean heal him."

"I told you the token bag is broken. I have no power to do anything beyond what my fucking character became during this incarnation."

"What were you?" Troy asked.

"A software programmer."

Troy called into the gray sky, "So all is lost."

I was ready to give both the dog and the trenchie the endings they both needed, but I had to find out one thing first.

"Why did you say you needed me?" I asked.

"My instructions were to get you to Portland alive."

"Why?"

"That's all I know."

"Yet you were about to kill me."

"You pissed me off. I don't like that Fr—— po—— shit. See, I can't even say the words."

I should have known better than to spend my time talking to the captive instead of watching where the boat was heading. We hit a rock in the middle of the damn river, and it took on water rapidly. It was time to go.

I jumped over the side and swam for the Oregon shore.

Troy shouted after me to at least untie him, but I was too far away to do anything about it. Troy and Kurtz howled in horrible unison into the dark afternoon sky over the dark river of the dark land.

Portland, tomorrow at noon. Monique.

My clothes quickly became sodden, and I knew I wouldn't make it to shore in such cold temperatures while wearing them. So I stopped and treaded water long enough to kick off my pants and unbutton and shed my shirts.

Just a man and his dick.

By the time I got to the top of the hill, the sun was setting. The sun was setting, but the snow had stopped falling.

I went over the top and down the other side. Down through the fir forest and into the darkness of night.

I couldn't think of the word that described how I felt. It wasn't "lonely." I never minded being alone and in conditions most people complain about as being lonely. Hell, just the day before I had staked out my own little Time Closet just to get away from it all. Now I was away from it all even without the Time Closet. That hadn't happened often. Usually z popped up and kept me occupied for a time when things were most bleak.

I wouldn't call the feeling "despair," That was a word for z and Eloise and John. They knew much more about the machinations of the infiniteverse and the ramifications and consequences of the dissolution of the Manifold. I didn't know enough to feel despair. Even with all my experience I hadn't moved much past "Be yourself." I'm not a big picture kind of guy, so I cling to what I know. Maybe that's why I'm one of the best at what I do.

Then I realized what the word was: Forsaken. And then I knew the feeling had not derived from my separation from z, nor from the loss of my token bag, nor from the hopeless situation in which I found myself. It was because I felt like I had been abandoned to the trenchies. How close they were getting!

Is it possible to lose faith after so many incarnations and Assumptions? I had never had much faith in the so-called system. But if the system was falling apart, if the Manifold was dissolving and the trenchies flooding through the cataracts, then perhaps I was forsaken by the very limitations of my superiors that I had previously always dismissed as quaint color. No, not intentionally forsaken, but forsaken by default.

Abandoned to the trenchies. That's the feeling that was coming on. Forsaken and abandoned.

But I had never lost faith in myself. "Be yourself" was too deeply ingrained, and my experiences had hardened into inviolable reality—regardless of whatever was trite and artificial in that slogan.

So I continued down the hill. I continued down the hill, through the forest, naked and alone, and feeling forsaken by everything except the one thing that mattered most: myself.

Then around midnight, I made it to the bottom of the hill and found a highway.

Cold and tired, beat down by the sensations of human fatigue and frailty, I waited for a vehicle to pass by.

A semi barreled down the near lane. The trucker honked his horn at me when his truck's headlights lit up my naked pasty flesh before he sped off with his haul to points unknown.

No one will stop for a naked freak on the side of a forest highway at midnight.

I moved to the far side of the road and began walking east. Toward Portland.

As cars passed me, I put out my thumb, but to no avail. I'd never hitchhiked before. I wasn't sure I was doing it right, but then again, I couldn't imagine how you could do it wrong.

I came upon a sign that showed it was 45 miles to Portland.

Portland, tomorrow at noon. Maybe it's already today.

I decided I would walk the whole way if I had to, but then I heard the exhaust brakes of a semi rumble through the night, approaching me from behind. *z?*

No, not *z*. Things were far too wrong in his world at the moment.

The semi slowed as it pulled past me, and it stopped in the middle of the road. It had an enclosed plain-white trailer and the sleeper was huge. I thought about Hera, Athena, and Aphrodite. This could be a good ride.

As I climbed into the cab, the warmth embraced me like Aphrodite had under the heavy quilts in the hold of the *Potemkin*.

"You okay, buddy?" the driver said. At that moment I wasn't in my right senses to judge anything about the features of a human being, but looking back I could swear it was the body *z* had inhabited only two days before. But all I noticed at the time was the faded yellow CAT hat he wore.

"Where's Cooter?" I asked.

"Cooter? I ain't know no Cooter. Why you naked?"

I slammed the door and the driver started off down the road.

"I had an accident."

"I didn't see no car on the road."

I shivered and rubbed my arms vigorously to try to make the warmth penetrate faster. Penetrate. I usually would make a sexual joke about such a word, but my mind was as numb as my body.

"It was on the river."

The driver looked at me and screwed up his face. He couldn't fathom my situation.

"You ain't human, is you? The river's five miles over them hills and it's near freezing out."

Maybe he could fathom deeper than I gave him credit for.

I simply laughed and said, "If I ain't human, I don't see why it has to hurt so much."

Ain't? When did I last say 'ain't'?

"Got some clothes in the sleeper. Probably a little big for you, but will keep you warm all the same."

I crawled into the sleeper and was disappointed to find it devoid of hot goddesses. I found a duffel that I thought was full of clothes, but instead it was full of pot and cash. I could feel the driver's eyes on me through his mirror. Why he had a rear-view mirror on a truck with a sleeper attached was beyond me until I saw that the back wall of the sleeper was wallpapered with centerfolds. At that moment I was the one who felt like a centerfold, and I was drawing too much attention to my crack.

Then the truck slowed.

I looked for clothing of any kind, but found none. But damn, the blankets were warm, and I wrapped one around me. I was sluggish and didn't think too clearly about anything other than how warm I felt. Only a faint sense of danger arose when the truck pulled off onto a side road. We drove on for a short time, and I began to feel better. The problem was that when I began to feel better, I began to think better. And when I thought better I remembered better. And all I wanted to remember when I could remember better was her. *Bitch.*

The truck came to a stop. My sense of danger was clearer by then as well, and it was strong enough to prompt me to look for some kind of weapon.

The two-foot pipe with the electrical tape wrapped around one end like the tape on the handle of a baseball bat would do nicely. After all, isn't that what truckers keep such a club for anyway?

The driver had that greedy look in his eyes that I've seen from z in the men's shower at the local gym. But I knew this guy was not z—at least not today. It was only then that I notice the faded yellow CAT hat was actually yellow ochre. For all z's shenanigans, the one thing he held sacred was his work against the trenchies, and he would never play games with yellow ochre. Besides, it didn't suit his season.

The driver began to undress. He took my huddling under the blanket as compliance. I let him undress. No, I had no interest in seeing him naked. It's just that I wanted him to do the work of removing his clothes. You ever try to remove the clothes from a dead man?

When his pants were around his ankles, I struck. The pipe clanged hard against his head, and the skull give way under the blow. I had done that once before in the battle of Agincourt. It wasn't all longbows you know. How do you think we killed off the French after we'd shot the horses out from under them? Teach them to write such poetry.

And best of all, I had crushed his skull without drawing blood. Nothing to hide. Nothing to hide but a body.

I put on the clothes and sat in the driver's seat. The truck was deep in the dark woods on a minor service road with no place to turn around. Either the trucker was a moron, or he knew the service road had an outlet. Maybe both.

I put the truck in gear and set off down the road.

After fifteen minutes, I came to a large gravel lot in front of a row of three tin-covered Quonset huts. A few broken down semi tractors were on the far side of the lot with weeds growing up between the chassis and rear wheels. Rusted parts were strewn across the yard. A collapsed trailer container leaned against the last of the dome-shaped buildings.

The yellow ochre flag flying above the door of the middle hut told me all I needed to know about this facility. I stopped the truck and dumped the body in front of the trenchie field station. That relieved any worry about human law enforcement.

As I pulled through the lot, three men in yellow ochre trench coats exited the first hut and shouted something I could not hear over the sound of the truck's engine at full throttle.

"It's go time!" I said. And this time I meant it literally. Go. Get out of here.

At the highway I was ready to turn toward Portland. Only thirty miles to go.

Portland, today at noon. Monique.

Fuck Portland. Forsaken. Yes, warm now, but still forsaken. Where's *z*? Only trenchies, and a whole hell of a lot of them. I wondered what a Time Bomb on that facility behind me would do to the whole scheme of things.

Be yourself.

Really? And where had that gotten me? Alone. Forsaken. Abandoned. Following orders and only finding more trouble.

To hell with it. Neither noon tomorrow nor the Brooks Range on the Solstice. They can have it. Time to go rogue and let them catch up to me if and when they can.

There was only one person left I could trust. Me. And it was time to go talk to myself and sort out what to do next.

I pulled onto the highway heading west. Away from Portland. Away from my duty. And hopefully away from all those fucking trenchies.

Chapter 8

The miles had blown past me as I'd driven out of the night into the early morning, the subdued glow of the pre-dawn sky was purple on the cookie cutter ridge of the Coast Range east of me. As I'd pressed further away from Portland, the yellow ochre had ebbed. No longer present. No dead-eyed gaze. Nothing.

Finally.

I'd taken Highway 101 south at Astoria. I'd only stopped once near Depoe Bay. Had taken a walk down in the pitch black of the night to the pier in search of the *Potemkin*. No dice. Just the empty berth and the smell of the ocean and death and night cold. I'd resumed driving.

More or less.

Each turn of the rig was followed by a resounding thump from inside the trailer behind me. A loose piece of cargo? Maybe. I would need to take a look. Could be something useful. I'd already gathered what little junk that trenchie driver had left in the cab, which wasn't much beside the weed and wad of bills.

I was fading. The monotonous lull of the road was taking me down to the void of sleep. Just north of the California border, a Wal-Mart beckoned in the fading dull of night. Morning was near. It was time to stop. I pulled the rig in and parked among the other trucks in the glare of the lot's lights. I killed the engine and crawled into the sleeper, keeping the pipe next to me. I'd take my chances.

On my back in the sleeper's cramped bed, I stared up at the ceiling. I was exhausted, but could not find sleep.

Eloise.

I'd never see her again. I was done. Done with all that. I'd made my choice, cast the die, set things into motion. I was abandoning *her* now. Not *quid pro quo*, not spite on my part: rather, sheer exhaustion. Perhaps she'd forgive me one day. Perhaps not.

I wanted her. With me. Now. I'd finally been able to admit that, but that's the way the infiniteverse arrays itself. You can't always get what you want. Didn't I know it.

The Manifold is dissolving, z had said.

There was no chance of making my flash point now. None.

From where I sat, I was now trapped in this incarnation. Abandoned. No Eloise. No z. No Assumption. Forsaken. No ticket out of here. No one to take my place and free me. Alone to the end. Like John had been those many days ago before he had been unceremoniously shot and put in the ground.

Without my token bag, I felt pain now. I was naked. Defenseless. Only I would bear my wounds, bear my burden, more so than I'd ever done. I was tired and had bad breath and still smelled like that swill of a river I'd crawled out of hours ago.

I drifted into sleep as the deep red burn of the rising sun slowly pushed up over the Range.

I rolled over on my side and closed my eyes.

The sweet peace of sleep.

The sweet peace of Eloise.

I always hate this part of a funeral, Michael had said.

Had John's funeral been a week ago when he'd said that?

I'd always had a grasp of time. Truth-time varied, but I'd been able to feel my way through it by fighting the boredom, the tedium. Ticking off the days of the week, the weeks of the year. Until the flash point and the jump.

Now, I lay on the bunk of the truck's sleeper with the rain pounding on the roof. I took one last drag from the joint before pressing it into the ashtray, the blue smoke curling around my hand. Why were the trenchies so uptight if they smoked that shit? It was some primo stuff.

I was losing my hold on how many days had gone by since the funeral. This was new. My grasp of time, gone.

You're still coming to bowling on Tuesday, right? Michael had said just before I'd left the church post-funeral.

I laughed, exhaling the smoke of the joint with a cough. "Like that's going to happen, Michael."

No, those days were gone. The good old days when the three of us palled it up in Vegas and the Valley. Software development. I'd done a lot of crazy things in my previous incarnations, but software development was the gravy train. The shit was dead easy to do and the money just kept rolling in. The conferences. The women. The travel. I'd gotten used to it.

I had woken in the truck at noon. I looked at my watch — just past two o'clock. I wasn't in any hurry to move on. I just wanted to stop for a while. But, I needed to piss. Bad.

I opened the cab door and climbed down to the ground. I tucked my shirt into my pants. These clothes were too damn big. The rain poured down.

I walked across the parking lot to Wal-Mart. I took a piss, picked up some groceries, and a knife. Not as good as my knife, the one in the bag, but it would have to do.

A woman's voice blared over the store's intercom. "Greetings Wal-Mart customers! We just want to remind you that this store will be closing at six p.m. today so our associates can enjoy Christmas Eve with their families. Merry Christmas from Wal-Mart!"

A wave of calm recognition flowed over me. I wasn't sure if it was from the weed, or if it was real.

Christmas. Tomorrow was Christmas Day.

I checked my watch again. If I drove straight through, I could be in San Francisco tomorrow. Be there by Christmas Day. I could find him. I could talk to him. He would understand. I would have to get there before he…

"Is that your truck?" the young petite auburn-haired cashier said.

I turned around, my eyes following her finger. She pointed across the parking lot to my rig on the edge of the lot.

"Yeah," I said. "That's mine."

"Thought so. I saw you walking in," she smiled. "Saw the banner on the back of the trailer. I'm a huge fan of the show!"

I nodded. "Uh, thanks."

She had the most creative pick up line I'd heard in a century. Over the swell of her right breast, her nametag read "Aymber" with a hand-drawn smiley face.

She handed me my change. "Merry Christmas and God's speed! Thanks for shopping at Wal-Mart!"

"Excuse me, miss," I said.

"Aymber," she smiled an even bigger smile.

"Aymber," I said. "Nice name. Where can I find a station that sells diesel?"

She'd given me her phone number as well as directions to Cooter's Diesel Plaza and Truckers All You Can Eat, where her brother worked. I'd given her a wink and the implied promise of a phone call. Perhaps yes, or perhaps no. With all lost, the idea of having some three-cent pancakes with a bit of Aymber syrup appealed to me.

I walked out of the store and back into the rain. The effects of the weed had fully kicked in and I demolished the box of Twinkies between the store and my rig.

As I rounded the back of the trailer, I stopped dead in my tracks. I hadn't noticed it before, the big bold letters painted across the trailer's rear doors:

The Man in the Dark Trench Coat Express – He's Coming! Soon!

I threw the groceries in the cab and found a set of keys with a handwritten scrawl on a piece of tape that read, "Padlock."

I've got to see what the fuck is in that trailer.

I keyed the lock. As I released the tall door's latch, it occurred to me that the cargo might be alive and wearing yellow ochre. And now pissed since they'd been in there for over twenty-four hours. I found the knife and, as discreetly as I could—considering I was stoned and brandishing a knife in a Wal-Mart parking lot near Brookings, Oregon—I swung open the back door of the trailer. In the rain.

The grind of metal-on-metal roaring finally stopped when I had the door fully opened. In the dim light of the Christmas Eve late afternoon, I peered into the trailer's dark recesses. Not much cargo at all. I could make a couple of black snow-mobiles and four or five crates near the front. Nothing alive, human or otherwise.

I climbed into the trailer and walked toward the front, my feet echoed with each step into the black. The snowmobiles were of no use to me, but I looked them over anyway. One crate was marked "Destroy upon receipt." I broke open its wooden lid with a couple of stomps of my boot: books of French poetry. Minor works only. *Figures.*

I turned and jumped back when I saw the black casket. I'd missed that on my first inspection. I drew the knife and slowly moved to the lid. Did I want to open it? I held the knife up in very dramatic fashion (thanks, D.H.) and threw open the lid. No body and nobody. Rather, lying in the center of the bed of the casket was a heavy plastic tube about four feet long. I picked it up.

I slammed the casket shut and sat down on it and broke the seal on one end of the tube. Inside was what looked like a rolled up piece of fabric. I pulled it out and opened the roll. It was a painter's canvas.

The painting was a bit tacky for me, but the nude woman who was the subject of said painting was pretty hot looking. I didn't know why the artist had made her wear the fur coat, though. That was my main criticism. And, yes, I had been an art critic once.

My other issue was the yellow ochre backdrop behind her. It'd never been my color. Ever. That was over. Perhaps I'd fetch something for the painting in San Francisco. They love shit like this. I rolled up the painting and slipped it into the tube. I tucked the tube under my arm and went through the rest of the crates.

I found nothing of much utility in the remaining crates. A few trinkets which I'd stuffed in the duffel bag that had belonged to that trenchie trucker. I kept the tube with the painting beside me in the cab.

I found Cooter's Diesel Plaza and stood next to the truck as the attendant filled the diesel tanks. San Francisco by tomorrow. He'd be at home that day, that much I knew.

The rain continued to pour. I paid, and then I fired the diesel engine up. I was down to fifty bucks. Shit.

Just before I turned back onto the highway, I was stopped by a passing hearse and a procession of cars.

Yet another death. Yet another funeral.

The procession passed and faded into the rain. I turned the rig out onto US 101 and headed south for California.

* * *

It all went back to John's funeral. The nexus. The single foci.

More or less.

John had told me of his cancer a month before. Had said it was terminal and he had only a few weeks left. "I'm dying, Mitch. Real death."

"You'll be Extracted," I'd said. "You know the drill."

"Not this time," he'd said. "I'm an indirect. I can feel the Flow in me. You can feel it. I know you can. I offer you a gift. Channel me."

After that, we'd 'togethered' into the early hours of the morning. Had I felt guilt over this? Not really. He had been a narcotic, an addiction. A temporary exit from this incarnation.

A flash of yellow ochre had been here and there in the days before John's death. I'd thought the signs were for me. Flash points aren't exact. Never have been. They're subject to the ripples in the Manifold like everything else. The yellow ochre had been early for me, but nothing to write home about.

I'd seen similar signs as Michael and I had driven to the church for John's funeral. I'd told Michael that I'd never been to a funeral where anyone looks forward to it.

Truth was I'd never been to a funeral of another Time Walker. A Walker who'd not made the flash point and the jump. Or, who hadn't dissolved in front of me during the Extraction when their brief had ended prematurely.

No, this was different: a Time Walker who'd died like *they* do.

The whole idea of it had been farce. John dead? Not just the physical body of the incarnation, but John...gone? The final exit?

Prior to the service, the minister had talked to me about John and God. He'd been rehearsing his bit for the eulogy. He'd asked me how well I'd known John.

The Nave had been empty. No one could speak.

God. As if that Factor came into the picture.

Then, Aunt Jenny had shown up. Always reliable, always the guardian of the Sardonics and the purer faith. Yeah. That Aunt Jenny.

She'd found her way through the throng of mourners and sat down in the pew beside me just before the start of the funeral.

"You really fucked this one, Mitch," she'd started, her voice low and controlled. "What the hell were you thinking? You were here for him! That was your brief. To make sure he stuck to the plan. That bullet was meant for you. Not him. What made you commit this, this felony?"

I sat and said nothing. Why bother.

"z told me all about it," Aunt Jenny had said. Her eyes had been moist. "Your last jump. Your violation of the standard protocol. And now this. John. Gone. I never pictured you as a renegade, Mitch. Never. Didn't think you would toy with the Void."

"John told me he was tired," I had said.

"Tired. Is that all?"

The minister cleared his throat. The service had begun.

"We're here to remember John," the minister said. "Please take your seats."

"I suppose I must rise to the occasion and say a few words," she had whispered to me as she'd waved her hand toward the people in the pews. "For *them*. Make some vapid remarks about 'fantasy football' or 'that he was a good kid.' To comfort *them*. Death is real to them, Mitch. John's death in this Truth-Time is a tragedy. You've got his blood on your hands."

"Don't you think I know it?" I had said. "Fuck!"

She had rolled her eyes. "Keep your voice down. You're in a place of their worship. Have some respect. Especially for the dead. I'm pulling you out, Mitch. Now! You should already be seeing them. The signs. The yellow ochre—"

"I'm not due out for another few days—"

"Save it. For all I care, they can have you," she said, "but, z said you still have some value. This time, just do what the hell z tells you to do. Okay? There's more afoot now than even your philosophy will allow. You've set a thing into motion. It's now beyond you. The tragedy of it. You were supposed to take the bullet for John. The Extraction had been set for *you*. Not him. We couldn't get him out once it happened. Nice work, Mitch. Nice work."

"I always hate this part of a funeral," Michael had said.

What I'd kept from her, the thing that I wouldn't reveal, was that John had told me to let him take the bullet. To let him go. Be gone from all of this. Not just the trivial incarnation.

Something else entirely.

More or less.

* * *

It was early afternoon when I found myself sitting on a bench near the underside of the Oakland Bay Bridge on the east side of San Francisco. The sky was so crystal clear blue that you lost yourself looking up into it. It was Christmas Day.

I'd made my way to my old apartment. Just off The Embarcadero in the shadow of the bridge. I'd remember. Slowly, at first. Sometimes the previous incarnation is a mere shadow across the tapestry of the infiniteverse. It takes time to access the shadows. To fully pull in the grasp of a memory from what had once been my here and now. In each incarnation, you'd be stuck in linear time. You only had what you came in with. Nothing more. Nothing less.

I hadn't seen a trenchie since I'd killed that son of a bitch near Astoria. No ochre. I'd had to ditch the semi near Eureka. I'd heard the CB chatter; the CHP had been looking for a stolen long bed. One that had been carrying "valuable" cargo. The one I'd been driving. I'd caught the red eye bus from Eureka into San Fran, blowing the remainder of my cash on the ticket.

The Embarcadero. The memories washed back on me as I sat overlooking the bay. The road lined with palm trees. The lights of the Yerba Buena Lighthouse across the still waters of the Bay on those warm summer nights when I'd sat on my second story balcony smoking cigarettes and pot and drinking tequila.

Yerba Buena. *Clinopodium douglasii*. I had my own herb to trade. I needed the cash.

I'd come back in search of the one person who knew me. Knew how the nagging death hung with me. Hung with him. In all that mattered to me, he knew it all. It used to be that souls and the afterlife were fairy tales for me. They didn't matter. Didn't even register with me.

Now, I wasn't so sure.

Doubt. I was unable to empty my mind of it. It came back and haunted me with every shadow in the corner. Every hint of yellow ochre my mind had cast over the rolling hills of the city. The bay was quiet today. I was quiet.

"You look lost," came a voice from behind me.

I turned my head. He was younger, some ten years my junior. I knew it. His jeans, faded and full of holes. *The look.* I'd always told myself at his age. *That look.*

"I am lost. Lost and forsaken," I said. I turned back to the bay. The lovely familiar bay. The memories were coming back full now. Ebbed in on the rising tide. I could recollect the smell of the grimy water. The call of the gulls overhead. The roar of the traffic on The Embarcadero.

"Melodrama. Not what I'd expect. You don't do it that well," he said. He sat down on the bench beside me. "Why are you here?"

I chuckled. "I've been wondering that very thing for a week or more now."

He frowned. My frown. "Don't get philosophical on me. That's not exactly our strength."

"It's the Manifold," I said. "Something's wrong. I can't channel the Flow anymore. Can't access anything."

"I've sensed something," he said. "z was just telling me that—"

I turned to him. "I can't get to the bag."

His body stiffened as if I was infected with something that I might pass on to him. He moved his hand to his side. He was checking.

I looked away. "Do you still have our astrolabe?"

"Yes," he said.

"Good. That's good."

"You look like shit," he said. "You smell like shit. Come on up and get a shower. My clothes will fit you. They always do. I also want to know what's in that tube you're carrying."

As I stood up, I caught the flash of a truck on the Bay Bridge above us. The truck that was mid-span, heading into the San Francisco side. The truck I'd been driving and had abandoned.

Only now it was yellow ochre.

They weren't here for me. They were here for him. For what I would ask him to do for me in the coming hours. For what I'd set into motion through him.

"It's a painting," I said. "Let's go."

Chapter 9

The alarm clock near the bed showed 11:59. Almost midnight. The room was dark. The bed warm. He had liked the painting while I hadn't. That struck me as odd, but he was the art critic after all. He had accepted it as his Christmas present. One minute left of Christmas day. Less, actually. He reminded me of the Christmas we had experienced long ago, but we laughed when he pointed out it had actually occurred in the springtime.

His gift to me? Well, I'll keep that between him and me.

A moment of comfort. An evening of comfort and warmth and uplifted spirits. The more human I became, the more I appreciated those human needs.

The alarm went off. *Midnight.*

He looked at me.

"And those Ancient Greeks thought they were so advanced," he said with a furtive smile.

"I'm hungry," I said, "I'm getting nervous, and that makes me hungry."

"You'll think clearer on an empty stomach," he said.

"Speak for yourself."

"I am."

We got out of bed and went to the kitchen. He made me a couple slices of toast and two eggs over-hard. *Just the way I like them.*

"That will tide you over," he said, sitting across the table from me with nothing to eat or drink. He simply sat there with his hands folded in front of him on the table. "Your reflexes seem to have slowed enough as it is."

I savored the eggs. Just the right amount of pepper.

"Why you so nervous anyway?" he asked. "You said you needed cash, I'll get you your cash."

"We don't remember everything, do we?"

"Depends on whom you mean by 'we.' Remember Zamyatin? If you miss your third flash point, you're stuck in your human body and will age with it until the trenchies get a hold of you and make you one of them. Open and shut. Sardonics 101. You'll continue to forget details of your incarnations until nothing remains."

"Don't you fear what ramifications this has for you?" I asked him.

"No."

"Why not?"

He answered, "I adhere to one principle and one principle only. 'Be yourself.' Remember that one?"

"But if—"

"If nothing!" he said. "z and Eloise and Aunt Jenny and the trenchies and Rufus T. Eisenstein and the whole galactic cluster fuck can go to hell as far as I am concerned."

"But the Manifold," I said.

"Have we been certified to give a damn about the Manifold?" he shot back at me.

The eggs were good. Damn good eggs. I could give a damn about these eggs. But why did he serve grape jelly instead of strawberry jam. Not everything added up.

"What?" I asked. I couldn't seem to follow him all the way. Was it human fatigue, or just...God, I can't even keep up with my own thought here.

"You have one principle you've been certified to follow, right?" he challenged me.

"Be yourself," I repeated as if from the catechism.

"And you think because you touched the Void or because John or Eloise went renegade and explored the Void without authorization that the entire fucking metaphysical structure of the infiniteverse will come crashing down? What makes you think things are so fucking fragile as all that?"

I said, "z, and Aunt Jenny—"

"How often have they screwed us on our incarnations, our Assumptions, and our Extractions?" he asked. "Why do you think they invented the mini-flash if not to correct their own fuck-ups?"

He had a point. I mean of course I have always felt such things, but never really had someone I could rely on to share my suspicions and make them meaningful to my own existence—that is until now.

He continued, "And what makes you think Aunt Jenny is the be-all and end-all of the whole infiniteverse? What about Cronos and Uranus? Maybe she's been spending too much time fucking her bastard cousin Rufus T. on the other side of the Void in her begonia garden and has neglected her precious Manifold and then turns around and blames you just because you were a naughty boy and touched what you weren't supposed to touch. Scapegoat. You and John and Eloise."

I had forgotten I could be so forceful. It had to be the human age. Maybe I'm losing my grip. Maybe I always lost my grip at the end of an incarnation and simply always forgot about it by the time the next one started.

"I'd like some coffee to wash down the toast," I said.

"You think you're nervous now? That caffeine won't help you any."

"Give me some fucking coffee," I said.

He got up and brewed a pot. He had inspired my own sense of forcefulness.

"We need to meet him in the Castro District at one. We'll have to hurry," he said.

"We'll hurry," I said. "But you don't remember everything either, do you?"

"I'm sure I don't," he said. "Memory is gaseous, not solid. You don't see what's missing. The memories that you do remember fill in the empty spaces so it always seems that what you remember is everything. Sufficient and complete. But there's always room for more. And for the creative Time Walker, you can always invent your own memories. Why do you ask?"

"If you remembered everything, you'd remember why I'm so nervous," I said.

"You're not scaring me into being nervous. Of the two of us, you're the one most likely to be wrong."

He doesn't know about the bus. Probably better that way.

"And you're the one most likely to neglect something important," I said.

"I take what comes," he replied. "All I need to remember is to be myself. You'd make us both feel better if you took that to heart and forget Aunt Jenny and z and the supreme guilt trip they're putting you on. You aren't responsible for the Manifold, goddamnit, and if you missed your flash points, it's because you were being yourself and everything will end up okay in the end. And if not, if the Manifold is dissolving and the infiniteverse is falling apart, it's not your fucking fault, okay?"

"But I did touch the Void."

"And what did you feel?"

"Nothing. It was the Void."

"And remember Aunt Jenny's cousin Eve. Remember what she said the apple tasted like?"

It was beginning to come back to me. From the beginning.

"Nothing," he said. "Big promises of knowledge and wisdom and discernment, but nothing. That's the big secret right? That all the lofty mythology reduces to nothing, right?"

I had not remembered ever being so nihilistic.

"And I'm not being nihilistic," he said. "You still have to live and eat and sleep and fuck. That's all still fucking meaningful, and it's probably all that is meaningful. I'm just saying all the codswallop they feed you about things you aren't certified to understand is better left to those who are certified to understand them."

My energy was ebbing and flowing. Waxing and waning. Coming and going. He would grab me at one phrase and I'd let go at the next.

The coffee was ready. He poured me a cup and handed it to me. He said with a sneer, "Liquid courage."

My self-loathing was palpable. I took a sip. I felt better.

"You've been in touch with the Olympians, haven't you?" he asked.

"You seem to be reading more and more of my mind," I said.

"The longer we're together, the more I understand."

"Why do you care about the Olympians?"

"Zeus and Eve were always the two most reliable of Aunt Jenny's cousins," he said. "Their clans can't really get involved, but they're not above a little minor meddling. I'm telling you not to count on them to get you through this."

"I'm not," I said.

"But take whatever help you can get," he said.

"I do."

"So what are you going to do?" he asked me.

"I'll decide after I get the cash."

"You only have one thing left to do."

"What's that?" I asked.

"The last thing you were instructed to do."

"Meet Monique in front of the Portland Art Museum?" I said, shaking my head. "That was supposed to be yesterday."

"If she's doing her job, she'll still be there," he said. "She's a persistent bitch."

"You know her?"

"I know her kind. She'll continue to keep an eye out for you."

"And the trenchies?"

"Don't worry about them. They told you they weren't out to kill you."

"Probably something much more nefarious," I said.

"Just go meet Monique. *z* says she has something to give you, and she'll also tell you what the trenchies want from you."

"It's almost one o'clock," I said.

"You still nervous?" he asked.

"Yeah."

Damn, I should tell him about the bus.

"We'll take the bus," he said. "It's go time!"

* * *

The first time I met Aunt Jenny was after my tenth incarnation. Ribbons for making tenure. I was overwhelmed by the ceremony. Mt. Olympus was a different place back then. Not a bare mountain in the north of Greece, but a heavenly abode. The ambrosia was delicious, and Aunt Jenny was so proud to show off her prized pupils to the other side of the Titanic family: the Olympians and the Edens.

"What the hell are you doing?" he cut in.

"I'm remembering," I said.

"I need you here with me," he said.

"But it helps make the time go faster."

He slapped me. The smack echoed throughout the empty bus.

"Who gives a damn anymore about Aunt Jenny?" he said, "Isn't my company more important to you than that? Isn't our time to be together running short? Hesiod and Moses and Buggerman. Leave the storytelling to them."

He had a point.

"I'm trying to avoid thinking about something," I said.

"You're afraid something is going to happen on the bus, aren't you?"

I didn't have to tell him after all. Should have know he'd remember it for himself.

"Just a feeling I have," was all I could say.

He slipped his hand into mine and squeezed it. Comfort. He held on tenderly for a moment then let go, never to touch me again, but I felt a sudden release of all the infinite burden that had built up inside of me since—since when? How long had it been building?

He looked at me and spoke more gently than I had heard him speak all night, more gently than I could ever remember speaking in my whole existence. "Since Eloise left you stranded, Mitch."

Eloise Potempkin, bitch extraordinaire.

"Not stranded. Forsaken. And I've let go of her," I said.

He did not believe me, and I did not have the energy to explain it was my decision and that I would stick with it until the end of Truth-time. Whatever that meant anymore.

The moment was drawing nigh. I gripped the back of the seat in front of us. The tableau developed as we rode the bus through the Castro District. It was just as I remembered seeing it in my dreams. The fallen lamppost. The two male whores at the front of the alley, one holding a dog on a leash, the other actually somewhat attractive. The advertisement on the billboard touting the flavor of Golden Delectable apples from the state of Washington, even though I was sure the one in the photo was contraband.

He was right. Time was short. And I had one more thing I had to ask him. But he was already ahead of me.

"I don't know anything about mom, Mitch," he said. "I don't know anything about what happened before the first incarnation or how we got through our first twenty years. You'll have to remember that for yourself."

He had cut through the question-and-answer session to save time. For even while he spoke, the figure in the yellow-ochre trench coat got on the bus and sat down in the front seat. Once the bus was moving again, the figure approached, just as in my dream.

Mitch had the duffel next to him. The duffel of pot. The tube with the painting in it stuck out from the mostly closed zipper. It had been too large to carry entirely in the duffel bag.

Mitch seemed to have no qualms about what was approaching.

The figure in the yellow ochre trench coat sat down across the aisle from Mitch.

Next he'll stand and bury the dagger into Mitch's—

The figure in the yellow ochre trench coat stood, but instead of wielding the dagger, he held the duffel bag. He pulled the cord above the windows and the buzzer rang. He got off the bus at the next stop.

Next to Mitch, in the aisle, was another duffel bag. Mitch handed it to me. In it was enough cash to get me anywhere I ever wanted to go and keep me there for as long as I wanted to be there.

"You had nothing to be nervous about," he said. "I told you that your memories were most likely wrong."

I looked at the figure in the yellow ochre trench coat walking into the night just as he discarded the tube with the painting against some rusty trashcans.

"Wait!" I yelled as I pulled the chord above the window. The bus had already begun moving, but stopped suddenly, throwing us forward against the seat in front of us.

"Don't worry about it, Mitch," he said.

"Your Christmas gift!" I exclaimed.

"It ain't Christmas anymore."

I jumped over Mitch's legs and up the aisle before the bus could take off again.

Outside on the sidewalk, I took up the tube with the painting. I popped the plastic cap on the end and pulled out enough of it to be satisfied that nothing was wrong with it.

Mitch stood beside me. The bus had moved off down the street. It was dark and it was night and it was quiet. I wished it would rain.

"Go to Portland, Mitch."

I clasped the painting to my chest. It wasn't my style, but I felt as close to it as I had felt to any woman. Any woman except—no, any woman. I put the tube in the yellow ochre duffel bag of cash.

"Maybe I should lie low with you for awhile," I said.

"Go to Portland," he said.

"I was wrong about the bus," I said. "I don't want to leave you."

"You weren't so wrong about the bus," he said. "Only in the details."

"What do you mean?" I asked.

But he did not answer. Instead, he stepped out into the street in the path of an oncoming bus. I still hear the sickening thump to this day.

Before I could move to help, I noticed the driver was decked out in yellow ochre and then a flood of yellow ochre-clad figures poured out of the bus and surrounded the body lying in the street. But before they could get their hands on it, the body dissolved into the street, and they were left with nothing but fists full of empty clothes.

The machinations were still in order. No matter how bad things might be, no matter the state of the Manifold, someone had managed to extract him. Sometimes premature withdrawal is a good thing. Maybe there was hope after all, despite his doubts. Maybe even enough hope to get me back on my 'be yourself' pony. And after all, hadn't I really been there all along?

* * *

The trenchies left me alone. I slept in his apartment, his bed, and ate his bacon and his eggs for breakfast. By noon I made it to the train station without any interference, and the yellow ochre creeps avoided my car, my empty car. My solitary, lonely, empty train car. They avoided it, but I could feel them in the rest of the cars on the train.

Along the way, each time the railway ran near the freeway, the semi I had come to know so well was faithfully prowling along at the same speed. I wasn't going anywhere without them. I hoped Mitch had been right about Monique. I had a ton of questions for her.

I never let go of the duffel that contained the cash and the precious painting. I clutched it to my chest with my arms through the straps.

We cut over to Sacramento and then up the valley, over the shoulder of Mt. Shasta, and into the Siskiyous.

Trenchies. The last stop in the great chain of being. Time Walker misses the third flash point and the trenchies get a hold of the human in which the Time Walker is stuck. One-way trip, no going back. No way up the chain, only one-way down. You just spend your life trying to keep the *status quo*. Mitch had been right. Sardonics 101. And when you die as a trenchie, only oblivion awaits. Non-existence. The end of the line. Only as they teach it, once you're a trenchie, you're so far gone intellectually that you are oblivious to the oblivion that awaits. You just chase after the nearest Time Walker with hopes of feeding on his memories without fear, without dread, without despair of what awaits once the inevitable end comes.

So why are they so passive? Do I begin to even doubt the fundamental nature of Sardonics 101? Or do they adhere to a power that someone of my pay grade is not certified to know about? Certification. Look what happened to Eloise and John who sought out the knowledge without certification. Or did anything really happen to them?

And what did Eloise mean that she would sacrifice her life to get me to the flash point? Sacrifice her life? Miss the flash point herself and become a trenchie, or something more abrupt, more traumatic. Direct annihilation? And what exactly did she fear happening if she didn't get me to the flash point? And if it is all so important, why the hell did she—no, I don't give a damn about that anymore. What does z mean by the Manifold dissolving and the trenchies pouring through. And John. John and the Flow. It is all too far beyond me. All I know is that I never experienced such a difficult transition into another incarnation, so whatever was happening was more dire than anything Mitch could contemplate. In his youthful cockiness he wouldn't have grasped the situation anyway even if we had been certified for more than 'Be yourself.'

I woke up. I had been dreaming. No more questions. No more doubts. The one remaining idea was as alive as it had been when I crawled out of the Columbia River how many days before? *Portland, tomorrow at noon. Monique.* Be yourself. Forget why the trenchies are being passive. Just be thankful they are. Deal with what comes next when it comes.

Then it came. Just outside the dreary, proper logging town of Roseburg, on a ridge overlooking the Umpqua River, around midnight of a moonless night, the embankment gave way and the train plunged into the river.

I was thrown from the car and found myself embedded in the mossy and muddy bank of the river. The duffel remained clutched to my chest. I did not move for a long time. In the darkness, the wreckage groaned as it settled against the rocks of the flowing water. I listened for footsteps. I listened for voices. I listened for any kind of organic activity. Nothing.

I moved a little at a time. First my arms, then my feet, then legs. My shoulders and head. I was okay. Nothing broken. Nothing hurt. Just damn scared. Had the trenchies set this up?

I slowly rose to my feet.

Up from the shore of another river. Up another embankment.

I felt the plastic tube with the painting. It was unharmed as far as I could tell.

If the trenchies had set this up, they had sacrificed five train cars full of their number to try to pull it off. Or had the machinations simply continued to work in favor of the earnest and devoted Time Walker?

Up the embankment. Over the railroad tracks. Further up the embankment. It's much easier to do when appropriately dressed for it. I even had a jacket this time.

Portland, tomorrow at noon. Monique.

I'd have no problem getting to Portland. One of the locals would get me into town by morning, and a bus or truck or even small plane would get me to Portland in time to meet Monique.

But you can become a believer in the Flow once more, and its ever-present grace, when events exceed even your wildest expectations.

As I mounted the shoulder of the highway, a Cadillac Escalade idled on the opposite shoulder. The dome light lit up and showed the silhouette of a familiar form.

Aphrodite!

I ran across the road and opened the passenger-side door.

"Need a lift?" the blond goddess asked. She had been playing *Words with Friends* on her tablet with Hera and Athena.

I kissed her. "How did you know I would be here?"

"Part of my job. Part of my promise, you know?" She winked at me. "You did pick me, remember?"

"How could I forget?"

"You'll find some clothes in the bag on the back seat," she said.

She put the Caddy in drive and three hours later we were in the Benson Hotel in downtown Portland. We didn't even see the semi anywhere on the freeway.

She was gone when I woke up, and so was the Escalade, but she had left me detailed instructions on how to find the Portland Art Museum. Maybe I wasn't so forsaken after all.

I walked to the museum, my duffel bag in tow, and arrived an hour early, so I headed across the street to what looked like a low-key family pancake house called The Three Little Kittens. Turns out it was a strip joint, but the guy at the bar said he could set me up with a full platter of seventy-four-cent sausages.

And so I feasted.

But when the doorbell tinkled and the woman entered, everything changed.

Chapter 10

"Of all the strip clubs in all of Portland she walks into mine," the guy at the bar said in the midst of handing me yet another plate of chipotle tripe sausages.

I took the overloaded plate from him. Forsaken or not, I was starving. "Keep 'em coming, chief."

"Yeah," the guy said. He looked clean over my head at the 'she' who'd just walked into The Three Little Kittens. I sat at the bar with my back to the entrance. The barkeeper's rapt gaze told me all I needed to know.

The 'she' the guy had referred to was probably a beautiful woman in yet another bar in yet another city. After last night's...issue...with Aphrodite, another beautiful woman was the last thing I wanted to see.

I didn't even bother to turn around.

"Sal," she said. "Been a long time."

Her voice had an indistinct accent. Familiar. Vaguely familiar.

I shoveled half a tripe sausage into my mouth. At least the 'she' wasn't Aphrodite. Don't know if I could face her again. Not after last night. At the Benson, in her penthouse suite. Hard to hold it against a man when a goddess is involved, right?

At one point last night, Aphrodite had stood up and frowned at me. "I've never had this happen before, Mitch."

"Figures," I had said to her. *Happens to the best of us, right?*

117

"It's alright," she had mused as she had slipped on her robe. "It happens. To mortal men of your age. Or so I've heard. Although, it's the first time I've experienced it, I must admit. Kind of makes me wonder what the true extent of my powers are."

And now *this*. My body was sore. The long hot shower this morning had done nothing to ease the pain. If only I had the token bag.

If only.

Sal leaned both of his meaty hands on the counter. "What brings you here, Monique? I thought you were better than The Three Little Kittens. That's what you told me when you left."

I held the sausage in mid-bite in front of me. *Monique*. What were the odds? I hesitated for a second or two. Then finally shoved the rest of the greasy sausage in my mouth.

I pointed to my coffee cup. "Hey Sal. I need something stronger. Whiskey."

Sal frowned at me as if he was swatting an irritating fly. "Serving time starts at noon, bud."

"It's eleven-thirty," I said. "Come on. Just make it thirty minutes short of a full shot."

He paused and looked at Monique. He then took my cup.

I finally turned around on my barstool. Monique still stood at the door. The questioning look of determination was on her face. She was here to meet someone. She glanced at her watch: designer and bespeckeled with enough carats to give a rabbit...

Monique was indeed beautiful. Dressed in a pair of tight jeans, boots, and a leather jacket that seemed molded to her body, tracing every curve and rise of her long and tall upper torso. Her shoulder-length straight blonde hair, upset by the cold late-December Portland wind, wavered around her young face.

Her eyes locked on mine. She raised her eyebrows and moved with no hesitation to the stool next to me.

I was good at guessing the age of a person. An occupational hazard, so to speak. She was at most thirty-two.

Sal shoved a teacup full of an amber liquid in front of me. I could immediately smell the whiskey's alcohol-laden fragrance. A draft from the front door of The Three Little Kittens blew on my back. Someone entered.

I was cold. I took a sip.

"Bonjour, Mitch," she said. *"Nous devions rencontrer en face du musée."*

She slipped onto the barstool to my left.

I turned to her. *"Anglais, s'il vous plaît. Mon français n'est pas très bon.* Please. I'm tired."

"Sure," Monique said. "Mr. Pimpkin told me you preferred French."

I laughed and stabbed a tripe sausage and held it out to her. "A sausage for your thoughts?"

"You're early," she said. "Coffee, please, Sal. Black."

"Actually, I'm late by a few days," I said. "But, I love this place! Sal is such great company."

Her gaze. "You're early for our meeting today. I got a call last night to meet you. Here. Today. Before time runs out."

"That's funny," I said, turning to her. "Not too long ago I would have remarked how irrelevant that statement really is in our line of work. Now, it means something."

She was a Time Walker. I hadn't lost that ability. Yet.

You just knew, that was the crux of it. Knew when you were in the company of your fellows. Would get together when the brief allowed a meeting. Have a few beers. The usual.

I saw it when she removed her red knitted scarf. The tattoo. A small discreet tobacco-colored marking on the inside of her left wrist.

"Interesting tattoo."

She didn't even flinch. "We all do things against our better judgment for someone we love. You know that more than I do."

"True. Truth. Time. That word, that word! 'By that sweet ornament which truth doth give!'" I said. "Save it, Eloise. It's not working."

She raised her eyebrows. "Eloise?"

My face flushed red. "Sorry."

"John told me you were prickly," she said. "But, you know Shakespeare. And, there's a woman who obviously means something to you."

I leaned back in my stool. "John. That was a lifetime ago. A lot of water under the bridge since then. But, who cares now? Not me, honey. I don't give a shit about us. Or them. Or her."

"That might be your problem, Mitch," she said. "You won't stick your neck out for anyone."

I clapped. "Nice performance. You act?"

"I do theater," Monique said. "Small stuff. So far. But one day—why are you looking at me like that?"

I slammed down the whiskey in one gulp.

"You remind me of someone," I said. "From a few decades back when I was in Virginia. A lifetime ago. She was a thespian, too. And young. Like you."

A scowl crossed Monique's face. "Fuck that emotional shit. We've got a brief to finish, Mitch."

I shoved another sausage in my mouth. "Was it something I said, or are you on the rag?"

"Whatever, Mitch. I've got to use the ladies room," she smiled a curt smile and stood up. "I hate being a man's memory of another woman."

I knew what she meant.

* * *

I opened my eyes.

10:00 am.

I'd cleared the jump. Made the Assumption.

I was in a bedroom. The room was hot, stuffy. I rolled over on my back, the sheets sticking to my sweaty thighs. The bed I was in smelled of a woman. She, however, was not here. Outside the window, a heavy fog drifted by.

I got up, nude, and stumbled to the bathroom, the disorientation of the jump still surged through me. I stood and took a long piss, then gazed at my reflection in the bathroom mirror: I was young; I was twenty; again.

Whatever that meant.

I splashed cold water on my face and looked around. Judging by the womanly paraphernalia in the bathroom medicine cabinet and scattered over the counter, I was the guest here.

I stretched. My cock was still hard from my morning piss erection. I loved this time in my brief. The hubris of youth. The strength of it. The randomness and newness of it all.

I went down the narrow hallway to the kitchen-cum-living room of her apartment. It was hers, alright. I was the visitor. I had found a small drawer of my stuff in the chest of drawers near the bed. Underwear, shorts, a few t-shirts, condoms, my pipe. That kind of shit.

I drew open the living room curtains. No sun. Just the fog. The tacky thermometer outside the window read close to eighty degrees.

She'd left a read newspaper on the kitchen counter. I picked up the front section:

June 6th, 1984.

The 80's. Better than The Sixties, but how I hated this decade, yet I was back again. I left the radio off because of the pop tripe I knew I'd hear. Unless Renee Chaney was on and playing Chopin. Then, I might have a listen.

Coffee.

I rounded the counter and drifted into the kitchen.

A rolled up piece of paper protruded from a white cup next to the coffee pot. I pulled it out, and then poured a cup of lukewarm coffee. Microwave ovens were still cancer machines during this decade, so I didn't bother warming up the liquid.

I unfurled the note. It was a woman's handwriting.

> Mitch,
> Rehearsal should be over by four. Meet me at Tybalt.
> Dinner at Thelma's at six sharp.
> R.

I scrounged some breakfast and downed a couple of shots from a tequila bottle I'd found on the counter. I spent a few hours going through her place, looking for whatever would give me a bearing on this brief.

Her name was Rosaline.

I'd apparently just met her recently, so that was good. Not much else. She was a student at George Mason, and, from the stack of playbills, had done theater. Small stuff, mostly. Was on the pill too, and had a thing for black lace panties. Or, maybe that was my thing. Didn't matter.

I then took a long, cold shower in the sweltering midday heat.

As I drove north toward Herndon, the temperature was pushing ninety degrees. The fog had since burned off, and a few white puffy clouds roamed the sky. The moist hot air had me sweating like a pig. A Latin one at that.

I drove like a man in his twenties. I blew through stop signs on nondescript streets, *et cetera*, and eventually found the Tybalt Playhouse. I parked the car on the street and got out.

I walked up to the theater's entrance to find Cooter sitting on a stone planter swinging at bugs with a badminton racquet without strings.

"Aw, fuck," I said. "Been a while, Cooter."

Cooter waved and beamed a big smile at me. "Mitch!"

"Where is he?" I said.

Cooter pointed the racquet to the glass doors a few paces down from where I stood. He then proceeded to go after a grasshopper and spit out a string of expletives that made even me blush.

The theater's darkness pulled me in out of the heat of high-summer Northern Virginia. I pushed my sunglasses up and waited in the wings for my eyes to adjust.

I entered, and the whole of the seats and stage opened up before me. A player's voice boomed from the stage:

> *"In faith, I will. Let me peruse this face.*
> *Mercutio's kinsman, noble County Paris!*
> *What said my man, when my betossed soul*
> *Did not attend him as we rode? I think*
> *He told me Paris should have married Juliet:*
> *Said he not so?"*

"No! No! No!" came z's voice from the darkness. "Cecil, you must concentrate on this."

"What's my motivation?" Cecil said.

"Motivation? My dear boy you are Romeo! You've just killed Paris and are dragging him down in the crypt! Juliet's body is before you! I need more emotion from you! Begin, again."

> *"In faith, I will. Let me peruse this face.*
> *Mercutio's kinsman, noble County Paris!*

"Sit down, Mitch," z said. "Good to see you made it in one piece. We've had a problem with *that* as of late. Not to worry. The Techs say everything works just fine."

Cecil droned on. I knew bad acting when I saw it. After all, I'd done my share on and off the stage:

> *Come, bitter conduct, come, unsavoury guide!*
> *Thou desperate pilot, now at once run on*
> *The dashing rocks thy sea-sick weary bark!*
> *Here's to my love!*
> *O true apothecary!*

I whispered to z. "The apothecary could be the hero in this."

In the dark of the dimly lit theater, I felt z's scowl. "You sound like Cooter."

"Fuck you."

> *Thy drugs are quick. Thus with a kiss I die.*

"Much better, Cecil. Die more convincingly, please. Continue."

> *Saint Francis be my speed! how oft to-night*
> *Have my old feet stumbled at graves! Who's there?*

"They eat this stuff up," z said. "They don't understand the significance of it, but they feel the tragedy that is love and death. Unlike us, eh Mitch? We know why we're here. We know what our existence means."

"If you say so," I said. "I still don't get it. What's the point of it all? The point of the jumps? The flash? The brief? Not that I care one way or another."

"I'm assuming *that* was rhetorical. Really, Mitch, you must be careful making such blasphemous statements in front of me. Everything is in the Sardonics. *Everything*. It's the last word. You never did pay attention in the classes, did you. I don't know what to do with you at times. Ah, here is your Rosaline!"

Rosaline rose and stood up. Of course, she was beautiful and young and full of *it*. Most of us are when we're in our twenties. Her black hair was piled on her head in a clumsy bun. Her narrow waist and heart-shaped face. I was a lucky young man.

> *Romeo! O, pale! Who else? what, Paris too?*
> *And steep'd in blood? Ah, what an unkind hour*
> *Is guilty of this lamentable chance!*
> *The lady stirs.*
> *Thy lips are warm.*

"You see, my dear Mitch, they need this," z said. "Their lives are so devoid of life that they must create it on stage. Create a tragedy. They just live and then die. Spend each day just going on and on with it."

> *Yea, noise? then I'll be brief. O...damn... dagger!*

z jumped up. "Stop, Rosaline! 'Happy dagger,' my girl. It's not like you to drop a line. Especially this one."

"Sorry," she said.

She'd seen me. That's why she'd tripped over her line. Seen me next to z. I'd have some explaining to do, I guessed. Or, I'd just keep her guessing. I was still an asshole.

"Again from 'Romeo! O, pale!...'"

Rosaline cleared her throat:

Romeo! O, pale! Who else? what, Paris too?
And steep'd in blood? Ah, what an unkind hour
Is guilty of this lamentable chance!

"Much better," z said. "Continue."

He plopped back down in the chair next to me, then in a whisper: "All the world's a stage, Mitch, and I've been a player on most of them. One would say a performer, perhaps even a portrayer. Oh, here's the good part! Watch her magic!"

Thy lips are warm.
Yea, noise? then I'll be brief. O happy dagger!
This is thy sheath; there rest, and let me die.

Thunder boomed outside, rumbling the theater as well as my bowels. The theater went dark. A flash of lightning peeled into the theater from the slip of the entrance.

z stood and clapped: "Apparently, the gods approve of your performance, Ms. Rosaline!"

A surge of laughter and applause from the cast until Cooter came in yelling about the rain and the electricity and a now smashed frog. The emergency lights eventually came on.

"Well met! We open in two days," z said. "Let's call it a day and resume tomorrow."

As the cast disassembled, z turned to me. "They call this tragedy, Mitch. They need it. They breathe it. Makes their miserable little lives seem worth something."

"Then why do the two lovers both die at the end?"

z pouted a churlish grin. "What would you want? Romeo to wake up? The friar to take his own life with Romeo's dagger? Snatch it from Juliet's hand just before she's about to do herself in? Poppycock! What would be the point of it?"

"They'd live happily ever after."

"Now, Mitch," z said. "That is rubbish. Alas, you are young for this instant. For this brief. Ah! Here is your Juliet."

Rosaline came up the aisle toward us with a puzzled look. "You two know each other?"

"Yes," I said.

"Why didn't you tell me, Mitch?"

z smiled at her. "Now, now Rosaline. I've known Mitch for what to you would be an eternity. But, eternity is not forever. A friend of the family, so to speak. Isn't that right, Mitch?"

"Sure," I said.

"Well," Rosaline said. "In that case, won't you dine with us tonight? My Aunt Thelma does a mean gumbo."

I spoke up. "I don't think that'd be…"

"Dinner at Thelma's?" z said, beaming. "Why, Cooter and I would love to! The gumbo is probably better than Aunt Jenny's. Right, Mitch?"

I mouthed a "fuck off!"

"Great," Rosaline said. "I'll get my stuff. Mitch can give you directions."

I watched Rosaline as she walked back to the stage.

The one thing I was silent on, the one thing I offered no comment on, the one thing that had left my stomach in a lurch was the half dollar-sized astrolabe tattooed on the back of Rosaline's neck.

"Don't grow too fond of Rosaline," z said watching her glide onto the stage.

"You know me," I said.

z turned to me and stared. "Yes, I do indeed know you. And I mean it. Don't let it happen, Mitch. Especially this time," z's gaze wandered off over the cast of players. "Especially this time."

She came down from the stage and looped her arm in mine. She smelled of sweat and salt and woman. "Ready?"

It was over three months later when a mugger in yellow ochre Nikes pressed the barrel of his pistol against the base of my skull on a side street off Pennsylvania Avenue and pulled his trigger.

Then, darkness and the burn of the Extraction.

And Eloise's screams.

* * *

Back at The Three Little Kittens, I pushed the empty plate away from me and let out a long satisfying belch.

"I take that as a compliment," Sal said.

I looked at my watch.

Only God knows what women get up to in the bathroom. I have my ideas, but I'll leave it at that.

The glare caught my attention. The harsh glare of sunlight reflecting on windshield. I rose as the semi—the truck I'd been driving and had abandoned, the one that had been following me, the one that was yellow ochre—rolled by the street fronting the Three Little Kittens.

I ran to the bar and handed Sal the tube containing the painting. "Hold on to this for me. I'll be back for it."

Sal took the tube from me. "Hey, mister. You owe me for the chow!"

"Put it on my tab!" I yelled as I headed for the door.

And there, in the midst of all this, was Monique in the grips of three trenchies, being dragged to the semi.

I ran out of the bar.

"Goddamnit!" I yelled. "I'm going to lose another one!"

Then, the pain came. Only darkness this time. It wasn't the Extraction.

It was something hard slammed against my head.

I dropped into the abyss.

Chapter 11

I came to in the darkness with a splitting headache, but I knew exactly where I was. The damn semi had been appearing in my life far too frequently lately for it to be any kind of accident. The swaying, the stop and go, most likely on the freeway. I was enclosed in some kind of box.

Satin. A box lined with satin. Only as wide as my shoulders, and tapered to the width of my feet at the bottom. My head and shoulders rested on the most comfortable pillow I'd ever felt. Seemed kind of pointless, but appealing at the same time. At the very least you know that you'll be taking that last long sleep in comfort. I was in the casket I had seen on my first perusal through the trailer back in Brookings.

I pressed my hands against the lid, but it did not budge. Satin. I ran my hands across every surface they could reach. All satin. No escape lever. The age of Poe was long past.

I coughed. Traffic fumes. Fumes were actually a good sign. It meant the casket was not entirely sealed. I could breathe. I could put up with the noxious fumes knowing that life-giving air was also making its way into the casket. Traffic roared and screeched all around. The truck lurched and creaked on its way. Trenchies don't know how to drive worth shit.

"Anyone there?" I asked, expecting a trenchie guard to shush me.

A muffled female voice from nearby frantically tried to say something. I couldn't tell if it was a warning or commiseration. The slap echoed through the trailer. Likely a guard had taken the direct method in shushing the conversation.

A dull thud made my balls ache. The low moan and the sound of a body crumpling to the floor suggested the guard had been a male trenchie and had been incapacitated in the same manner experienced by all males of every species from the beginning of time.

"These guys aren't too bright, are they?" Monique said.

"Monique?"

"You're not too bright either, are you?"

I remained silent. *She knows me too well.* There was no indication she was doing anything to get me out of the box.

"You couldn't just go on up to the Palouse Range when you had the chance, could you?"

"Eloise said—"

"And who the fuck is Eloise, and why do you think her opinion trumps z's? She's just another two-bit hussy who gave you a hard on and blinded your eyes from Truth-Time."

"I just try to be myself," was all I could manage to say in my defense.

"And you didn't even try for Bombay which was clearly given to you as your second flash point. That bitch again throwing you off."

I said nothing for a long time. Then I started to get pissed. "Wait now. Who the fuck are you?"

"I'm Monique."

"I know that, but where do you get off busting my balls?"

"z's tied up at the moment."

"I've heard that before."

"Be serious, shithead. Don't you know the Manifold is falling apart?"

"I'm no fucking expert on the Manifold. Why is this all being laid on me? Hasn't someone thought to call Dr. Hodge?"

"Who do you think put us in this mess to begin with?"

"The way everyone's carrying on, I thought Eloise was the cause and I'm the one supposed to set everything right."

"Eloise was merely the proximate cause," Monique said, with special emphasis on *proximate*. "The first cause deals with machinations of beings far above your pay-grade."

"That leaves me as the final cause?"

Monique laughed. "You are simply the means. The service man. The boy who puts his finger in the dyke. Once you do your bit, the important people can begin to set things right."

"Dyke?"

"I gathered from your Permanent Record that the way to get through to you was through low, adolescent humor."

"Have you ever—"

"No personal questions," Monique said brusquely. I liked it when she spoke brusquely.

"So what did Dr. Hodge do anyway?" I asked. Monique was silent for some time. I called to her again, "Monique?"

"When was the last time you were in Sunday school, Mitch?"

I became sullen. "If you read the files in my Permanent Record, then you know I don't have any memory of my childhood."

"Enough of your whining pity-party shit. You know I mean Aunt Jenny's staff meetings."

"Aunt Jenny has staff meetings?"

"Shit, Mitch. Are you playing with me?"

"I'd like to," *Damn, and I really would.*

"What would Eloise say about that?"

"Why should I care about what that two-bit hussy would say?"

"Your Permanent Record says you're over the moon for her."

"First, what does *permanent* mean in our world?" I said. "And second, nothing like that could have been in my record because if it exists at all, it's too fresh." I had an insight: "You know her, don't you?"

"Fuck you, Mitch."

"Fuck you and that bitch, Monique. Now tell me about the evil thing Dr. Hodge did."

Monique began to weep. "Bastard," she said. I wasn't sure if she was talking about me or Dr. Hodge. Through her tears she told me the long sad story.

"He was Aunt Jenny's first love. He had discovered the prime law of Sardonics, the one we now call Hodge's law, and he used it to invent the Manifold. No more screwing around in the vacuum of empty space. All of us Time Walkers could inhabit the planets and ghistules of the infiniteverse and take the forms of and interact with the native beings. Do you hear me, Mitch! No more drifting in the vacuum of empty space!"

"I hear you, Monique."

"But then he found out that Eloise had passed Rufus T. Eisenstein's class on basic Sardonics by sleeping with him. Being a male, Dr. Hodge couldn't let a good thing go when he saw it. He gave Rufus T. a choice: total oblivion or keeping his mouth shut about the special classes the doctor intended to give Eloise—to make up for what she hadn't learned in class."

"I knew that bitch was putting it all on," I said.

"I think she understood the gist of it, " Monique defended her friend. "She had never been a good test taker."

"But she could score with the best of them."

"And what was your score, Mitch?"

"Didn't you read my files?"

Monique pretended not to have heard, "Dr. Hodge took full advantage of Eloise's precarious position."

"She does precarious positions?"

"You'll never find out, asshole. Rufus T. had always had a thing for Aunt Jenny, so he went straight to the Queen Bitch and told her everything."

I could imagine Monique flapping her hands and rolling her eyes and tossing her head as she expounded on the great gossip of the infiniteverse, forgetting I was just a dumb-headed man and not an eager sister of the talk. Next, she'd want my feelings on this matter and would be asking about Dr. Hodge's energy level.

"So Aunt Jenny kicked out Dr. Hodge," Monique continued, "and banished him to the other infiniteverse."

"There are two infiniteverses?"

"Dumb ass, everyone knows there are an infinite number of infiniteverses. But Dr. Hodge had more power than Aunt Jenny counted on. Oh, she won out all right, but the force it took to expel him from our infiniteverse left a vacuum, a wasteland, a nowhere in its wake between the two infiniteverses."

"The Void," I said, but she ignored my brilliant deduction. Likely, she was pissed I wasn't proving to be as dumb as she thought.

"Dr. Hodge threatened to undermine our Manifold and obliviate the Time Walker infiniteverse, leaving us nothing but the vacuum of empty space once more."

"And the trenchies are his minions."

"They are fallen Time Walkers," Monique said mournfully. "The ones he seduced into crossing The Void."

"But Eloise crossed The Void."

"No. Eloise *entered* The Void."

"So she broke the rules but not bad enough for banishment?"

"Bad enough for Dr. Hodge to get a foothold back into our infiniteverse and begin the destruction of our Manifold."

"If the Manifold falls apart, won't that leave Dr. Hodge and his trenchies drifting in the vacuum of space too?" I was getting the hang of asking these leading questions. But then she cut me down.

"Moron. Haven't you heard the rumors that Dr. Hodge has created a Manifold that connects all the infiniteverses into a single Omniverse? Once he destroys our Manifold, he will have control of the entire Omniverse."

"Seems unlikely," was the best I could come up with, then I sunk deeper into the shit with my next comment. "That sounds like the kind of tripe they'd teach in Aunt Jenny's staff meetings. Glad I never was invited."

"There's never been an invitation for anyone," Monique said in exasperation. "They are standing orders and have been effective since day one. Kind of like the scrum when you're playing rugby."

"Is that where you gather all your gossip?" I asked.

"It's where I learn the true nature of our fight to preserve our way of life, Mitch."

"So can you tell me, O wise one, why Eloise entered The Void in the first place? Why would our goodie-two-shoes, brilliant—but in a sleeping with the professor kind of way— bitch Eloise break the most fundamental law of Time Walking?"

"You just don't pay much attention, do you Mitch?" Monique said in a huff. I was not trying her patience on purpose; it just seemed to come naturally to me.

"I just do my job, Monique."

By that time I was glad I was enclosed in a protective container. Maybe those trenchies knew a thing or two after all, at least about the dynamics of gender relations.

"What are you implying?" Monique said.

"I'm not implying anything."

"Yes you are. You're implying that you hold yourself aloof from the daily drama of the other Time Walkers. You distance yourself and think you are too good for the rest of us. You think you are superior."

"That's what they said made me well-suited for my job."

"And you think I'm a low-life, feeding on the gossip and innuendo of the Time Walker break room?"

"Maybe that's why you are well-suited for your job."

The casket moved in a manner that could not have been caused by the movement of the semi in traffic. It was the movement of a large box falling to the floor and nearly splitting open, but it had been well made (probably in the trenchie infiniteverse) and I received no more abuse other than listening to Monique pounding on the casket trying to get at me.

When she seemed to calm down, I spoke. "So what is the juicy tidbit you wanted to share with me about Eloise and why she entered The Void?"

Monique must have been composing herself because she took a long time to answer, and when she did, she sounded as calm as she did before her outburst.

"Despite Dr. Hodge's obvious power play, Eloise had fallen in love with him during her special re-education sessions. After he had been banished, Eloise entered The Void to seek out the good doctor."

"But she turned back out of fear of Aunt Jenny?"

"No. She couldn't find him. She kept finding her way back to our Manifold instead."

"And each time she re-entered the Manifold, Dr. Hodge's reach across The Void grew stronger," I said. I was in rare form.

"Poor girl," Monique muttered in sympathy. "She loved him so much."

"That had to piss off Aunt Jenny even more than her violating The Void."

"You're so naïve, Mitch," Monique said blandly. She was used to it by now.

"I try to keep it that way, Monique. You have another secret about Eloise, don't you?"

"It's about Eloise and Aunt Jenny."

"You don't mean—"

"No, you pervert! I don't mean that. I mean that Aunt Jenny *is* Eloise. Or should I say, Eloise is Aunt Jenny's young-woman manifestation."

I had had enough.

"Monique, you're so full of shit. Next thing you'll tell me is that Dr. Hodge is Aunt Jenny's male manifestation or wait, maybe Aunt Jenny is a manifestation of her own self!"

Monique paused.

"You're a lunatic, Mitch," Monique finally whined.

"Now I don't believe anything you've said since I woke up in this box. All that crap went out with Spinoza. You're just regurgitating substance, attributes, and modes under another name."

"What does some troglodyte like you know about Spinoza?"

"Spinoza was my gig. You want to know the real reason I was ostracized from the Talmud Torah congregation of Amsterdam?"

"Knowing you, it was probably some sexual deviance."

"The chief rabbi's wife," I confessed. "She was one live wire. My question is, what does some pretentious slut like you know about Spinoza?"

"Hey, mister, I took all three sessions of professor Rufus T. Eisenstein's seminar on the Rationalists: Descartes, Spinoza, *and* Leibniz."

"I bet you scored well too—just like Eloise," I said.

What would Monique say if she knew Leibniz and I had our falling out because he couldn't keep his hands off my girl's monads?

"At least I know Spinoza died at forty-four," she said. "Just at the end of your tour, right? You kill them all off, don't you? How many human lives cut short because they had the misfortune of having you as their Time Walker?"

"He was scheduled to die at thirty. I carried him long enough to finish the *Ethics*. You would have learned that had you read my record with more care than you gave your schoolwork. Now all you have left are your myths and women's lounge gossip games. What good are they?"

"Don't you see how those stories explain everything? Can't you see how they clarify all your questions?"

"I don't have any questions. I just want to know what role I'm supposed to play to end this soap opera as soon as possible."

Monique's voice softened.

"You should have gone to your first flash point, Mitch."

"I didn't have a chance to."

"We sent Eloise to guide you. You abandoned her and she had to go off alone in that truck and do the best she could. Of course she failed without you there to help her. Now it all falls on you since you chose to try to make the third flash point. Always were a procrastinator, weren't you?"

"Hold on there, missy. You think I'm the one who abandoned her? She took off without *me*!"

"That's not how we saw it."

If her intent was to overwhelm me any further, it didn't work. In fact it relieved me of much that had troubled me throughout our conversation and indeed throughout the past several days.

"That makes me feel much better," I said.

It was her turn to be confused.

"Why do you say that?" Monique asked. "We've demonstrated that you were wrong. She was sent here to die to help you set things right, and now who knows what has happened to her because of your ignorance. She is likely dead already."

"You have just proven to me that you don't know as much as you think you do. Now I have reasonable doubt to doubt everything you say and fuck all the rest. I'm free again."

"Free to do what?"

"To be myself."

Monique didn't know what to say, so I continued. "You can have your trivial dramas and rumors and treacly interactions with others of your kind. I'll just be your service man and get that device from you and do what I'm supposed to do to save the infiniteverse and preserve your inane pleasures of the women's lounge."

"I can't give you the device, Mitch."

"Okay, then don't give it to me."

"Don't you want to know why I can't give it to you?"

"No."

"It's because that casket you are in is lined with lead. I can't access your token bag through the lead lining."

"My token bag is inaccessible anyway."

"Maybe to you it is."

* * *

The tattoos mean nothing. Not on a female Time Walker. They move around for optimum attraction for the male they are trying to either attract or signal—or both.

Monique had been hammering on why I'd intentionally missed the first flash point and all but ignored the second in Bombay, but something wasn't adding up. Her trite recitation of an obviously invented myth regarding Aunt Jenny and Dr. Hodge and the pending destruction of all we hold dear and sacred didn't make any sense. They know all of that stuff is lost on me. That's why I'm a field guy. Monique wasn't completely on the ball, but she thought she was. Definitely cut of the same cloth as Eloise.

The frequent references to the third flash point reminded me of the one other time I had failed to make the first two jumps. I told you before it was for a dame. And not just any dame. The kind of dame you would not only sacrifice your life for but would turn your back on the rest of existence for just one more night, even hoping that her last act at dawn would be to devour you whole like she had done with every other man before you.

Even Time Walkers are not immune to such compulsion. And considering she was a chief rabbi's wife, well, that just made the compulsion even stronger.

No one has ever spoken of it, and we all have played along like I did the right thing in the end by making it to the third flash point. But I did not have the power to resist her on my own. And truth be told, I knew she was a trenchie from the beginning. I only ignored all the subtle signs until that suitcase full of yellow ochre dresses left no doubt. But even then, I would have gone into that great mystery of seduction and destruction of my own free will.

Someone had to have intervened. But nothing was said in the debriefing. They played it like I had heroically managed to get to the third flash point under extreme and tragic circumstances. The oldest trick in the book. When you want to hide a screw-up, manufacture a hero. Come to think of it, I'm one of the most heroic Time Walkers I know.

No one has said anything or made even the slightest subtle suggestion that things were otherwise, and nothing deviating from the official story ever appeared in my Permanent Record. Far be it from me to seek out details of the weakest moment of my career, but someday I expect someone will expose to me the machinations that went into prying me away from my temptress.

Funny thing is, I don't even remember what she looked like. The power of the connection was so much deeper than the superficial appearances. It was simply a total longing for self-destruction in her arms.

I am not ashamed to admit it. I am just glad I was saved and was able to continue my service as an earnest, if not obedient, Time Walker.

At least they aren't trying to lay the blame for the pending destruction of the Manifold on me and my one true-but-hidden blemish. Now would be prime time for someone to create a scapegoat, or at the very least use it as leverage against me. On the other hand, maybe they really do depend on me to save the infiniteverse.

* * *

Finally, the semi came to a halt. I heard the back doors of the trailer open, and Monique squealed. A struggle ensued, but as far as I could tell, enough trenchies were around to subdue even this tigress.

The casket clattered around the trailer as they fumbled with it. They had as little grace in emptying the trailer as they had in driving it. Fortunately, the casket was not only lined with lead, but it also had ample padding under the satin fabric. The finely appointed interior had already saved me from suffering when Monique had intentionally fumbled the casket. Now I was saved again during the oblivious fumbling of the trenchies.

The lid of the casket raised, and I found myself in a warehouse. Monique was already tied up in a chair with another chair backed up to it. I wanted to kick her as they dragged me over, but they tied me up before I had the chance.

"Bastard," she said.

"Whore," I said.

"Asshole."

"Bitch."

"Idiot."

"Teacher's pet."

"Slacker."

"Busy-body."

Then a familiar voice filled the warehouse.

"Okay, children, enough fun."

And from behind a service door, Troy Marlow stepped out, and his dog limped along beside him.

"Who's that?" Monique asked.

"Troy Marlow," I said, in utter amazement.

"And you are Monique and Jim," Troy said.

"His name is not Jim, you idiot," Monique said, still on full throttle.

"Any man who would abandon a pilgrim ship in distress must be hung with the albatross of a name like Jim."

"You're mixing metaphors, moron," Monique said.

"Not metaphors, my dear," Troy said, drawing closer, "literary references." His face was disfigured from the episode in which I had left him for dead in the sinking boat on the Columbia River.

Troy addressed the crowd of trenchies that filled the warehouse.

"Where did you find her?" He asked his followers.

One of the trenchies that had abducted Monique answered: "In front of the art museum—as you guessed."

"And him?" Troy asked, pointing to me.

"He tried to interfere, so we brought him along too."

I was confused. "You mean you guys were after her all along, and not me?"

"She's the one with the device that can ruin our plans," Troy said.

"So where is it?" I asked.

Troy looked at his men. "Well? Where is it?"

"She didn't have it on her when we captured her," the talkative trenchie replied.

Troy was dismayed. "Come here, everyone."

Troy and his merry band of trenchies huddled to discuss matters.

"Where is the device?" I whispered to Monique.

"In your token bag."

"It's inaccessible."

"We've been through this before, Mitch. I have been authorized for temporary access."

"Prove it," I challenged her, knowing she did not like to be challenged.

"Look down," she said, undaunted.

In her hands was the dagger I had lent T.E. Lawrence for his photo shoot. The same dagger I had used to flay the truck driver who had tried to rape Eloise.

Our hands were tied near each other. I was just able to grab the handle of the knife and cut away, strand-by-strand, the rope that bound us to the chairs.

"Eloise has a message for you, Mitch," Monique whispered.

I didn't pay much attention, because I expected it to be more woman talk, lighter than air and not even substantial enough to pass through one ear and out the other. I kept focused on gaining our freedom.

"You're her Factor, Mitch. Her representative," Monique sighed like she was telling the dearest secret of the infinite-verse. "That's why Aunt Jenny and z and their superiors have put their hope—and the hope of all Time Walkers—into your hands. You have the device. I have done my duty. You are never to use it. You keep it safe for Eloise. And I mean it! Never use it. The consequences would be infinitely more horrendous than allowing Dr. Hodge to destroy our Manifold and create the Omniverse."

More big talk.

"Tell me, Monique. How many Omniverses are there?"

"Goddamn it, Mitch. There can be only one!"

"Did Dr. Hodge tell you that, Monique?"

"What?"

I cut through that rope and found that I had only managed to free my hand, not Monique's. I freed my other hand before one of the trenchies noticed my escape.

"He's escaping."

The trenchies began to circle us.

"Mitch, what about me?" Monique cried.

"I'll leave you with your friends," I said.

The trenchies moved closer.

I put my dagger to Monique's throat.

"What are you doing, Jim?" Troy asked in bemusement.

"Yeah, Mitch, what are you doing?" Monique asked, but without the bemusement.

I was in command. "Back off, all of you, or she's dead."

"What do we care?" Troy asked.

"You'll never find that device without her," I said, trying to remember the last time I tried to pull off such a blind bluff.

Troy held up his hand. "Hold it boys," he said.

I freed Monique from the ropes and pulled her toward the exit, the dagger pressed firmly against her throat. The trenchies parted to let us pass through.

"She won't tell you where the device is, Jimmie Mitchey."

"I'll get the device from her," I said, and I flashed the blade of the dagger at a couple of trenchies that came a little too close. They backed off.

"No you won't, Jimmie Boy. Only females of your species even know what it is, let alone can use it. You won't get far. Monique will track you down yet again."

I had reached the door and opened it.

"You can have her," I said. They approached the door, but just before they reached her, I slit her throat. Blood sprayed all over the trenchies.

"The device!" Troy yelled.

In one more movement of my arm, I severed her head and threw it into Troy's surprised hands. Her body fell into the arms of the trenchies. I ran. I ran far and fast.

I ran with fear and regret. Fear and regret, but also hope. Hope because I found that the warehouse was near the airport, and I still had time to catch the flight to Point Barrow on Portland Petroleum's bi-weekly flight.

Maybe I had done the right thing after all. I wouldn't know for sure until my debriefing—if we survive to have a debriefing. But I'm a Time Walker field man, and I'll live by my gut until my dying days.

Chapter 12

And I ran.

And I didn't look back.

And I didn't stop.

And I didn't witness Monique's Extraction.

I knew she'd been extracted, of course. It had to be so. The alternative was too...but, I was digressing. Or, she was indeed one of them, in league with them, and with all the bullshit she'd told me—it couldn't be otherwise, believe me, I know. That's what I thought. Otherwise I'd be guilty of a terrible— no, not now.

The first flakes of snow washed silence over the parking lot. The flakes were cold on my bare arms, my bare flesh.

I caught my breath. In the cold air, it steamed with each painful exhale. In the late afternoon dim light of the setting sun, my middle-aged body had finally drug me down. I'd slowed to a jog and slipped between two warehouse buildings.

I was now hunched over, my ass against the building's cold concrete. To rest. Just for a moment.

Marlow's boys were coming after me. I could hear them. Lots of them.

"Oh, Jim boy!" came a voice a ways from me. "Come out, come out wherever you are!"

My breathing steadied. I'd only covered some fifty yards before I stopped. I wasn't used to this type of running anymore.

But then the bullets began snapping near my head. No report from their pistols.

They must be using silencers.

Great.

That got me running again, albeit at a slower pace, and I zigzagged through the maze of buildings. I had to get out of there. Get to the terminal and get on that Portland Petroleum plane to Point Barrow.

I rounded the corner of the building, just missing a garbage dumpster. I stopped and ducked behind it.

Four rounds slammed through the dumpster's blue metal side opposite me. I needed to find some kind of weapon. There was nothing but open parking lot and runway and razor-wire-topped fencing around the complex of warehouse buildings out in front of me.

The gunman trenchie was nearby. I heard the heavy metal clunk of his pistol's clip as it hit the pavement followed by the snap as he loaded a full one.

I heaved the dumpster lid open. I frantically scrambled through the shit of the dumpster, pushing my way through bags of garbage and cigarette butts. Nothing. No luck.

Shit!

He'd heard me and, as he neared, the thud of his boots pounded closer with each passing second.

My hand ran into something solid. Something metal and cold and hard.

Finally.

I grabbed it and held tight, then pulled a bent pipe from the debris. One end was wrapped in electrical tape.

The trenchie rounded the corner, his pistol trained on me.

"Got you, Time Walker!"

I swung the pipe and bashed in the side of his head. He'd run right into it. His pistol skidded away from me under the dumpster and out of my reach.

He fell back and curled up on the ground beside the dumpster.

Without warning, the heat from him poured over me. The sharp crack of the shock wave blew me back and knocked me to the ground as the trenchie in a pure agonized craze glowed bright white.

The Calling!

The trash and debris in the dumpster shot straight up high into the snow-filled air. A vortex of shit hovered above me.

For a moment.

I rolled over and pushed myself flat against the building as the Time Wave crashed by me, the sharp prickle of its blue wake on my skin, the smell of his burning flesh, the distortion around the temporal Void hole that'd been the trenchie's body.

The Time Wave flowed over me. For a single fleeting instant, one single moment in Truth-Time, I could feel my token bag open next to me.

I could see it!

I could see Eloise!

A beat.

Then a flash.

The Time Wave washed past me and dissolved in a chorus of car alarms from the adjacent parking lot in the late afternoon of a dying sun and a gut-wrenching pound of distant thunder.

Then, all was quiet.

The airborne trash silently fell back to earth all around me.

The Void hole was gone.

And, the bag was gone.

Inaccessible. Again.

Truth-time had corrected.

My two other trenchie pursuers stood gobsmacked near the dumpster, their pistols dangling in their hands. They couldn't believe it either.

Time for me to get. As inconspicuously as I could, I crept alongside the building away from the two trenchies. They had begun examining the smear of what had been one of their own but was now just the smoking pavement from the Void hole.

As I came around the side of the building, a UPS truck pulled out from the loading dock. I gave one last heave of a run and just made the cab as the truck left the complex, the gate closing behind me.

The driver's surprised look and his yellow ochre eyes told me everything I needed to know.

I swung the pipe.

Then, I slammed the brake pedal and yanked the wheel right as his limp body slid out of the driver's seat.

The truck skidded to an unglamorous stop on the side of the road.

As I ducked to avoid the Calling, nothing happened. I wasn't sure whether that was good or bad. Back by the dumpster, I'd just witnessed the impossible. But, with a collapsing Manifold, what the hell was impossible?

I poked him with my pipe.

Nothing.

I drug his body to the back of the truck and drove to the terminal.

Sunset and snow. I parked the truck outside one of the terminal's delivery depots. I stood up and began going through the boxes in the back of the truck. Just my luck. I'd managed to hijack a UPS truck at Portland Airport that was chock full of quilting materials for shipment to the 54th Annual Quilters All Tied Up Convention in Tignall, Georgia.

All of the yarn was a strange tint of yellow ochre. I opened one last box, which was full of long knitting needles. I grabbed a handful and put them in my inside coat pocket.

Better than nothing. I couldn't traipse about the Portland Airport with a bent and bloody pipe. I'm good, but not that good.

I lifted the trenchie driver's security badge.

As I climbed out of the truck's cab, a single thought burned its way into my mind.

How does one get on an airliner to Point Barrow when one does not have a ticket?

* * *

I sat at the bar in the Alaskan Airlines Board Room lounge just off of the Portland Airport concourse. I pounded back the whiskey. I adjusted my hat, and then got the barkeeper's attention.

"Barkeep," I said. "Could use some service here."

I fingered my boarding pass in my coat's breast pocket. The lounge was empty except for a couple of men decked out in really expensive suits at the far end of the bar.

Earlier, I'd checked in with Julie, a cute redhead in a tight skirt, at the Portland Petroleum crew services counter and had bullshitted my way onto the Point Barrow flight.

The uniform had helped a bit. But a uniform always does. How I got it, well that's a long story, and I wasn't in the mood to elaborate.

She'd asked me how I kept warm up above the Arctic Circle. I'd told her it depended on how warm the woman in your bed was. She'd laughed and handed me my boarding pass and bid me to have a safe flight north.

I'd told her my bed was open to her.

She'd said she wasn't that warm.

Damn.

Now, I wait in this airport lounge, hoping to keep Marlow's boys off me for just an hour more until I can be wheels-up and out of Portland.

I popped another complementary jalapeno stuffer in my mouth.

The barkeep approached and leaned over the bar. "You flying today, first officer?"

I straightened my Alaska Airlines flight crew uniform coat. "Negative..."

I looked at his nametag.

"...Stein. I'm off duty. I'm catching a flight in two hours. Just killing some time."

"And brain cells..."

I laughed. "If you only knew the half of it."

Stein scrutinized me and poured me another whiskey. "What the hell, right? You guys fly all over the world. Work long hours like me. So, who am I to judge? Especially if you're off duty."

"Exactly," I said. "Cheers."

My token bag.

Back in the warehouse parking lot, I'd had it for a moment. I could actually feel and see the bag's opening just outside my reach. Then, it was gone.

The Calling. What the fuck? I'd paid attention to that part of the Sardonics. It was theoretically impossible.

I'd had my fill of theory lately.

Perhaps it'd been Monique's jump wave. I'd never seen the Calling before. No one had — so they say.

But, with a dicky Manifold, who the hell knew what was possible and what wasn't.

Made no difference to me, either way, which was what mattered.

I'd heard of the Calling from a guy in the Advanced Topics of the Sardonics training. He'd told me it's all mystical and shit, so I hadn't been interested in it. But, he'd said, no one had ever witnessed one. No one had because it was an impossibility. What the Calling represented was an idea abhorrent to a Time Walker. An errant Manifold. The breaking down of Truth-Time. And, reality.

Whatever.

The Manifold must really be fucked for this to happen. Probability-wise, the Calling is a non-event. A freak of the Manifold. An event never witnessed even by the Aunt Jenny crowd.

Yet, I'd seen it. I'd been inducted into an exclusive club.

More importantly, I'd felt the token bag.

I'd glimpsed the Void.

Stein snapped me out of my thoughts. "You doing alright, first officer?"

He smiled and then looked past me. His smile suddenly disappeared and he nodded to someone behind me.

Stein leaned over real close to me. "An associate of mine would like a word with you."

Panic, then I calmed myself. "Your associate got a name?"

"Oh, yeah," Stein said. "Marlow."

I jumped up.

Stein made a grab for me with his meaty hands.

I pulled out a knitting needle and jammed it down through his hand, pinning it to the bar.

"Shit!" Stein yelled.

I turned, but Stein, with his free hand, grabbed my shoulder, and then threw his fist into my chest, jamming me back down into my chair.

I struggled to get my breath back as he pulled the bloody knitting needle out of his hand.

He held me in the chair.

"That hurt," Stein grumbled to me. "Be nice, first officer, be nice. You're not a captain after all. You've run from your duty once. It's time to face your judgment. Time to be brave."

Marlow swept into the barstool next to me.

"Good to see you again, Jim," he said. "Nice to see you in uniform. Suits you."

"Name's Mitch," I said.

Marlow offered an apologetic bow. "Okay. Jim it is, then, Mitch."

I ran my eyes over to Stein, who shrugged, then back to Marlow. "How can you be in here?"

Marlow frowned a smile and winked at me. "It's magic, Jim. Let's have a temporary truce."

I nodded.

I acquiesced, actually. What the fuck else could I do?

Marlow motioned to Stein. The thug released me and moved down the bar to another customer saying, "It's okay. He's just had one too many."

"Be yourself." Marlow said. "The old Time Walker credo, eh, Jim? I was like you once."

I rubbed my hand over my now sore shoulder. "I doubt that."

Marlow lit up a cigar. "Nice number you did on that dame back in the warehouse. We had her marked. But, then she was Extracted."

I eased back in the bar stool.

"You look relieved, Jim," he said. "Don't be."

"Fuck you."

"What a mouth you have," Marlow said. "It's not pretty with that filth you're spewing."

There was a time in my career when I would have killed myself trying to figure out how in the hell Marlow was able to enter a bar. But, not any longer.

"I'm just being myself," I said. "Asshole."

"After you'd offed her, I was mad," Marlow said. "Really mad. At you. But then, the other event hit in the parking lot. My boys told me all about it. Suddenly, that made things very clear. *'There are men here and there to whom the whole of life is like an after-dinner hour with a cigar; easy, pleasant, empty.'* Words from the master. Words to live by."

"Fine," I said. "You fuckers can be a bit slow, can't you. I know why you're here. I saw it, too. Just like your...men."

Marlow took a long drag from his cigar. "I'm nothing but a feeble narrator. A teller of tales. But, this, this is magic! The Calling! You actually saw it! You're lucky, Jim. It's the stuff of legends."

I grunted. "You've never taken Aunt Jenny's Sardonics."

Marlow stiffened. "Ah, the great Aunt Jenny and her blind faith. Let me give you another perspective of the 'faith.' After the Calling, a trenchie is no more—"

"Standard shit, Marlow. Your point being..."

"Which is why you Time Walkers stay on the straight and narrow for the most part. The Calling is Ultimate Death. For any of our ilk. It's never supposed to happen. But, it just might, right? You see, that's the Calling's power: it introduces doubt that the Manifold isn't perfect. That it might be as fractured and screwed up as we are. That it and we, by extension, aren't perfection or good or bad or any of the other crap spewed forth by members of the 'purer' faith."

Marlow droned on and on, stating that for the few Time Walkers who actually see the *real* Truth-Time and come over to the trenchie side, the Calling is a sign of the Collapse.

"There's no return after it," Marlow said. "You simply no longer exist in Truth-Time. Nothing will."

He was right, of course.

"Enough with the lecture," I said. "It's not that easy."

"It is that easy, Jim," Marlow said. "It's you. I thought it was Monique, but she was blinding me to you. We'd had the wrong mark. We thought she was the one who would stop the Collapse. The Manifold is messing with us as well. It's all very clear now."

I emptied my glass. "Are we done?"

Marlow laughed and motioned to Stein. "Nice words, my boy. Finally! I will finally, finally be able to collapse the Manifold and then clean house. All will be better then."

I snorted a laugh. "You think that, but what of all this?"

I waved my hand toward the two men at the end of the bar. "What of them, big guy?"

"Let me give you another view of our struggle," Marlow said. "Time Walkers are an abomination. The arrogance of your kind! The hubris. Assuming bodies. The sin of it. You don't know the real damage you do to them. The Sardonics are not only for you. You're kind has fallen from the purer faith."

Stein filled my glass.

"I was never much good at the Tech," I said. I slammed back the drink. "Didn't do too well in the theory, either."

"See, you and I aren't much different, Jim," Marlow said. "We're just on opposite sides of the Sardonics. You need me as much as you need Aunt Jenny."

"Aunt Jenny," I said. "Don't get me started on that bitch."

Marlow was quiet. He glared at me.

In a sudden swift movement, he grabbed me by the neck and lifted me out of my seat. "Don't you dare, you insipid little Factor! I gave her everything! Everything!"

I tried to hit him, kick him, even spit on him, but to no avail. Finally, he dropped me back in my seat.

I rubbed my neck. "What the hell was that for?"

He refrained from hitting me, but I saw him form a fist. "She abandoned me," he said. "Left me stranded and all alone. She never came back. Just disappeared. I watched her go off. Never to return. And now look at me..."

With a wave of his hand, Marlow called Stein over, who proceeded to grab me again. That idiot Stein hadn't bothered to frisk me.

I pulled another knitting needle and pinned his good hand to the bar.

"Goddamnit!" Stein yelled.

I jumped up and punched him in the mouth, then buried another needle into his other hand.

Marlow grabbed me and threw me on the floor.

Stein pulled one of the needles out with his teeth. "Let me at him!"

"Easy, Stein," Marlow said. "All in good time. Bring him to me."

Stein pulled the other needle out, then brought me to my feet and shoved me toward the door, but not before giving me a head butt.

Marlow snuffed his cigar and walked beside me. "I said easy, Stein."

Stein's head butt had left me dizzy. That, or the booze. I couldn't tell.

They lead me to the glass door of the exit where Marlow's trenchies waited.

"Well, Jim," Marlow said. "I've enjoyed our chat. But, we really must be getting on with the business at hand."

"So much for the truce," I said.

"Please," Marlow said. "I'm a trenchie. What's my word worth, right? It's time for you to take your bullet."

Marlow opened the door.

The five waiting trenchies took me.

"Just keep one thing in mind, Jim," Marlow said to me. "I will stop at nothing, and I mean nothing to prevent your ilk from saving the Manifold from collapse. Nothing, Jim. You read me?"

"Ever heard of a god complex, Marlow?"

He ignored me. "Do not kill him, boys. Just tie him up. Make sure you use square knots. Our Jim is an able seaman. And can get out of most knots. There's been a change in plans, boys. We're headed as far away from the Palouse Range as possible. You're taking him to Alaska. You'll know fear, Mitch. You'll know it!"

How does one kill fear, I wonder? How do you shoot a spectre through the heart, slash off its spectral head, take it by its spectral throat?

Chapter 13

"So what am I thinking now, bitch?" I asked her.

She had been on the plane, tied up on a snowmobile in the cargo bay. They had dragged me past her, and she was already knocked out. They tied me up to another snowmobile, and then they gave me a shot that knocked me out too.

When I woke up, we were at cruising altitude in a Boeing 737 cargo bay somewhere over British Columbia. Eloise had been staring at me.

"So what am I thinking now, bitch?" I repeated.

"Hi, Mitch," Eloise said. She wore the same tight turtleneck she had worn when I saw her driving away in my truck, my jock around my ankles.

Eight trenchies guarded us. They sat nearby in airline seats installed in the cargo bay for the special purpose of providing seats for those guarding special cargo.

"When did they get you?" I asked her.

"Heading up into the Palouse Mountains. I didn't get far without you."

"I don't believe it."

The trenchies slept. They had no interest in our conversation.

"What don't you believe, Mitch?"

"Anything."

"Don't you want to know why I left you?"

"No. Fuck you and the truck you rode out on."

"It was for your own good," she said, but I wasn't convinced.

"A lot of good it did me," Those eyes were working their magic. I still didn't know which side she was working, but she was working all of me.

"I told you the Palouse Range was no good. We would have both been killed had we gone through with it."

"So you say," I replied. She would have to work harder than that.

"I told you the Brooks Range was the right place all along."

"Is that where we're headed?"

"Yeah. You're doing okay so far. Be yourself, right? Isn't that the credo you say you live by?" she said, her sarcasm was palpable.

"Why would Marlow and his goons be taking us to the Brooks Range if that's where we are supposed to go?"

"Dr. Hodge's orders," Eloise said confidently. "It's the single foci in this infiniteverse. Above the Arctic Circle on the Winter Solstice is when the single foci manifests itself and Dr. Hodge can leverage that to complete the collapse of our Manifold and establish the Manifold that will connect the infiniteverses into the Omniverse."

"Winter Solstice?" I asked in confusion. "I've already celebrated Christmas. How did we get back to the Solstice?"

"You know how things work, Mitch."

No, I don't always know how things work, but I have learned not to ask too many questions in such matters, especially of someone as pretentious as Eloise. No telling what kind of tripe she has bought into at any given moment.

I returned to the main point. "In any case, Dr. Hodge should want us as far from the single foci as possible—considering we are the only ones who can interfere," I said.

"He needs my device to spark the catalyst," Eloise said.

"Your device?"

"The device Monique put in your token bag to save for me."

I watched the trenchies carefully to see how much they were monitoring our conversation. They were dead asleep. I had run them through hell the past week, as they had run me through hell too. And back. More hell was sure to come.

"I understood I was just the courier."

"Your token bag was the only one we could disable to keep the trenchies out of it and yet still have access ourselves. Dr. Hodge has backdoor entry into the bags of all senior Time Walkers and above. You've saved the infiniteverse by never actually earning the promotion to senior Time Walker."

"Fuck promotions. And by the back door too."

"Now you know the real reason I entered The Void. I was sent to steal Dr. Hodge's Catalyst Starter."

"I don't believe it."

"You wouldn't."

"Bitch."

"Why are you so cynical and bitter, Mitch?"

I couldn't believe my ears. But then I didn't believe in much of anything even then.

"Do you want the whole catalogue," I answered, "or just the short-course?"

"We all have our problems, Mitch. Do you know what kind of hell I went through getting back across The Void and find-ing our infiniteverse again? Dr. Hodge set his diabolical plan in motion while I was still in The Void!"

"I don't believe anything you say, Eloise. Your metaphysics are wasted on me."

"I got the device to Monique just before I met you outside Moscow, Idaho."

"Why didn't you just give it to me in Moscow?"

"They would have captured it along with us. Aunt Jenny knew we would need to get it to you sometime after our first meeting."

"And now they have us and the device, and they are taking us to the location where said diabolical plan will be finalized—as I understand it."

"It is where we can end Dr. Hodge's ambitions," Eloise said. Then I recognized the self-important glow on her face. "I am the only one other than Hodge who knows how to use the device."

"Seduction has its privileges," I said. "So now you'll tell me that falling in love with Dr. Hodge was just a ploy."

Eloise ignored me. "By switching the polarity of the device, I can reverse the effect, destroy the nascent Omniverse and regenerate our Manifold."

"So you say. Take the device whenever you need it. As far as I'm concerned, I'm just there to make my third flash point. Let the chips fall where they may from then on."

Eloise looked at me in stunned disbelief. "You are incorrigible! Life as we know it is about to end, and you just sit there making light of it."

"What am I thinking now, bitch?"

"I can't read your mind, Mitch. Not like before."

"Why?"

"The Manifold is falling apart, shithead."

Then with that last word, it all clicked.

"That all you have to say, *Monique*?"

One of the trenchies opened his eyes.

"What are you talking about, Mitch?"

"Monique, Eloise, whatever name you want to use this time, it's fine with me."

"I'm Eloise, Mitch. Can't you feel it?"

"Then I feel that you were masquerading as Monique."

"Would you have fucked her as you said you would if you hadn't been boxed up?"

"Are you jealous of your avatar?"

"You've been with a woman since you were with me, Mitch."

"I never was *with* you, Eloise."

Eloise looked around. She was searching for something. The right word, the right feeling, the right something, but she couldn't find it.

"I played the part of Monique to fool them, Mitch."

"Sorry, Eloise. I don't believe any of it. I'm just trying to find my way to my third flash point. The rest be damned. And you and Monique with all the rest, including that bitch Aunt Jenny."

I watched Eloise carefully for any glimmer of personal offense. I never did believe Monique's assertion that Eloise was an incarnation of Aunt Jenny, but it's always good to test one's own hypotheses, especially when Aunt Jenny is involved. If she was Aunt Jenny, she didn't betray any sense of personal injury, and that's not Aunt Jenny. No, Eloise was conjuring another offense.

"You've had another since I saw you."

"Is that against the law?"

"I was beginning to love you, Mitch."

"Is that why you abandoned me across the street from Butch's Hardware store?"

"You've done alright for yourself."

"Something's going to happen, isn't it? Soon. No one's going to let Marlow take us all the way to Point Barrow by his rules."

"How do you do it, Mitch?"

"Do what?"

"I spend every nerve and fiber of my being trying to learn the ropes and live up to the standard of Aunt Jenny, and yet I always seem to fail when it matters most. But you, goddamn you bastard. You fuck off and don't give a damn, and know nothing about Sardonics and The Void and the Manifold and infiniteverse and Dr. Hodge's attempt to institute the Omniverse, and yet just by being yourself, you know just what to do at just the right time. Yeah, something's about to happen. Soon, just as you said. In fact, now."

And Aphrodite descended the ladder that connected the cargo bay to the main cabin above. Following her was none other than Troy Marlow, carrying his lame dog.

* * *

John left me.

If you want to know the truth, I did not measure up to his high expectations. He was more ambitious than I was, and he was always chiding me to get off my ass and buck for senior rank. Eloise also finds it disconcerting that I have such low levels of ambition. She calls it apathy. John did too. But they are wrong. Not that I can explain it, but there is a peace that comes from being yourself. Yes, I tell them that when they pursue their ambitions they are being themselves, and I have never condemned a single soul for chasing the vanishing promises of ambition. But I cannot explain why my course of action, or inaction according to them, is simply right for me. I don't seek to explain how things tend to work out for me despite my apparent lack of gumption. It is a simple fact, and a fact I will cling to and adhere to until I receive the comeuppance they swear is coming my way.

But after serving a thousand successful incarnations in the Time Walker corps, you would think someone would give me a fucking break.

That might be my biggest disappointment. John leaving me. He grew away from me, and he could not remain in Eden forever. He had his heart set on bigger and better things. I miss him. I don't know why Eloise has any interest in me beyond the fact that I was destined to be the courier for the device. In fact, maybe that is all she is interested in and she's using her seductive charms to keep me on point. She's not the type to trust a Time Walker who relies on being himself. No matter what she says about understanding this in me, she doesn't understand, and it drives her crazy. A Time Walker who relies on being himself is simply unreliable in her book.

John was much more her type. Shared ambition, a kind of superficial genius that attracts zealous followers and hot bodies for whom even one of the Olympians would die. Sure, they would annihilate each other once thrown together, but that kind of energy would light the infiniteverse for eons.

I have my place. I know my place, and I fill my place. I don't gripe or complain about it. I do wonder after our falling out why John was sent to be my indirect this time round. I wonder, but I don't go too far with it. It's not my thing to go looking too far behind the curtain.

It was nice to have John for even a brief time, but I couldn't forget the pain of him leaving me. He must have worked his way far up in the ranks to play the role of the human catalyst in the current drama. It was his death that sparked this thing in the human world. If we take Eloise at her word, maybe she did knock over the first metaphysical domino, but I know that bullet was meant for me, and John took it instead. It had been his brief, no matter what bitch Aunt Jenny says. I loved him, just as I loved David when my father Saul was king of the Israelites. John took the bullet for me, and that was the first physical domino to fall.

So he has left me again. Where they've assigned him since his Assumption, I don't know. Maybe they're saving him for late relief.

Yes, I'm developing a thing for Eloise, but I can't imagine it comparing to anything John and I had in Eden. Eden. Now there's a place for a vacation. When this is all over, assuming I can still stand the bitch, maybe I'll take Eloise to Eden and show her the sights.

John, where are you? In the beginning was John, and the word was with John, and the word was John. John. Make way the coming of John. Says John.

I'm a sappy drunk. I should never drink and write. If Eloise knew whom she had to live up to, she'd abandon me to the trenchies, just as she did outside Butch's Hardware. Then again, maybe that's her challenge. She gets off on such things. Is it possible she's out to conquer my love and overwhelm my nostalgia for John? John did outscore her on all the tests, but that was because he actually knew the stuff, not because he slept with Rufus T. John knew his stuff alright. And Eloise was pissed that she couldn't score better than he did.

She was Monique. Monique had read the files in my Permanent Record—so she said anyway. I'm sure it's buried there somewhere about my time with John in Eden. She's after me. She wants to get to John through me. I must be drunker now than before. Well, let her try. He left me, after all. Let her try her best. Nothing I could think to do would hurt him—punish him for leaving. I gave up on that long ago. Give her a go at it. I don't think it will do any good, but it will be fun while it lasts.

But I miss John.

* * *

"Baby, tell me how you got on my plane," Marlow begged Aphrodite.

"Tell me again why you are on this plane," Aphrodite said to Marlow.

"I've been ordered to transport these two Time Walkers and this equipment to Barrow, Alaska."

Aphrodite grinned. Then her grin turned into a big, beaming smile. "I like Alaska in the winter time!"

Aphrodite walked to the exterior cargo bay door and opened it. In an instant, Troy Marlow, his poor dog, and all eight trenchies were sucked out into the sky above northern British Columbia.

Eloise and I were safe, being tied down to secured snowmobiles. Aphrodite stood next to the cargo bay door. The drop in pressure had no effect on her. Her hair simply waved as though wafted on a gentle wisp of a summer breeze.

Aphrodite closed the door.

"Who's she?" Eloise asked with dark eyes.

"The one I've been with since," I said.

"I'm Aphro—"

"I know who you are, bitch," Eloise said.

"Is that any way to thank your savior?" Aphrodite said.

"My one and only lord and savior is Jesus Christ!" Eloise said earnestly. She had been president of Campus Crusade for Christ in her last incarnation. She had slept her way to the top, as usual.

"Cute," was all Aphrodite said. Then she looked at me. "Hi, Mitch."

I smiled. Eloise didn't like my smile, so I eyed Aphrodite from head to toe and everywhere in between. Especially in between.

"Nice to see you, Aphrodite. I'm sorry I was inadequate when we were last together."

Eloise sneered at me, "That's not such a surprise from a forty-five year old human male."

"It's okay, Mitch," Aphrodite reassured me, "You more than made up for it on dad's boat."

Eloise spit poison at Aphrodite, "I am his brief, cunt, leave him to me."

I laughed. I like to hear women use words with each other that they never let men use with them.

"I have come to fulfill a promise," Aphrodite said, and she draped an arm around my shoulder and kissed my cheek.

Eloise seethed. "What's this Olympian doing interfering with our brief, Mitch? They don't even have the right metaphysics!"

"Eloise, my dear," Aphrodite said lovingly. "We Olympians have discovered the nine-and-a-half feelings of emotional perfection. That is all the metaphysics we need."

"That's nothing compared to our five-and-a-half dimensions of Truth-Time," Eloise countered.

"I see you've learned your metaphysics by sleeping with Rufus T.," Aphrodite said.

Eloise was silent a split second longer than was natural for her. Aphrodite had scored.

"What's this promise you speak of?" Eloise asked. Non sequitur. She was reeling, but she did her best to hide it.

"I have a more important question," I said. "Did you take out all the trenchies on the plane?"

"Every last one of them," Aphrodite said with her golden smile.

"Even in the main cabin?"

"Every one, Mitch. Even in the cockpit."

"Then who's flying the plane?"

"It's on autopilot."

"And who will land it?" I asked.

Eloise had not taken her eyes off Aphrodite, but her gaze grew intense once more. She had recovered her footing and I had accidentally put Aphrodite on the defensive.

"I did not think of that, Mitch," Aphrodite said. But she still said 'Mitch' in a voice that pissed off Eloise, so I didn't mind.

"Goddamn you bitch, what will we do now?" Eloise was back to full throttle.

"Can you fly a plane, Mitch?"

"I flew with the Wright Brothers in Kitty Hawk, but nothing as big as this tub."

"You mean you really don't have a solution to everything?" Eloise shot at Aphrodite.

"What would you do, Mitch?"

"What would Mitch do? Is that all you can think of? This lazy no-account?"

"I would be myself, Aphrodite," I said with a smile as golden as I could make it, and saying 'Aphrodite' as much as possible in the way she had said 'Mitch.'

"How would that solve anything!" Eloise screamed.

"Things will work out," I said.

"Or they won't," Eloise said.

"Either way, something will happen," I said.

Eloise glowered at me. Aphrodite had removed my restraints. I was free. I kissed her deeply. She returned the kiss, but with merely a cousinly passion. She left Eloise tied up.

"What about me?" Eloise asked. "You going to just stand there and fuck, or will you set me free?"

"First, the promise," Aphrodite said, and she looked at me. "Mitch, I promised you the most beautiful woman in the world to be yours if you judged me the loveliest among my family. Now I have come to not only rescue you from the trenchies but also to fulfill my promise and give you the woman of your dreams."

"Me?" Eloise said with a look like she had just smelled the bottom of the laundry hamper after three weeks without being emptied.

Aphrodite kissed Eloise with the same cousinly passion as she had kissed me, and with that, Aphrodite was gone.

"Mitch, untie me," Eloise asked.

I was reluctant. Only moments before she had been full of piss and vinegar and bile and all kinds of nasty body fluids.

"Please," she said with a tear.

I untied her.

She stood and looked at me.

I looked at her.

"You chose me?" Eloise asked.

"Out of all the women in the infiniteverse, I chose you and you alone."

"Mitch, you know I must die. You know I must die getting you to that last flash point."

"Maybe in *your* metaphysics," I said. I caught a brief flicker of hope, a moment of doubt in her own mind about her beliefs, then it disappeared and her sadness returned. "No, Mitch. It must be."

"Then we will make these last days something for the poets to write about and young girls to cry about."

"But you could have chosen anyone else who was not doomed to die."

"I could have, but I chose you."

Eloise began to weep. She put her palms on my chest and leaned her head against me like she was listening to my heartbeat. I embraced her.

"Mitch?" she asked.

"Yes, my love?"

"What will we do about the plane?"

"Let's go have a look."

I led Eloise up the ladder into the main cabin. It was empty. The door to the flight deck was closed. Laughter came from within. Eloise and I looked at each other. I knocked.

"Yes?" came the familiar, squeaky voice in the faux British accent. "What do you lovers want, pray tell?"

"z?" Eloise and I said in unison.

Another laugh carried over z's. It was a maniacal laugh of a post-adolescent. It came from deeper in the throat, and was frantic in its joy.

"Cooter!" I said.

Eloise looked at me with a scrunched up face. "Cooter?"

"You know z," was all I could say.

I shouted into the door, "z, what's going on in there?"

"Now, Mitchey my boy, you know better than to ask questions like that."

"Who's flying the plane?" Eloise said, still concerned about our traveling safety.

"Damn it, Miss El, haven't you ever heard of auto pilot!" z said. And z and Cooter laughed and laughed and laughed their hysterical laughs until even Eloise chuckled a little.

I pulled Eloise deeper into the main cabin and we sat in business section. I kissed her.

"Not yet, Mitch," Eloise said, but she snuggled against my shoulder.

"Don't you want to join the club?" I asked.

"I'm already a member," Eloise said. "And besides, it doesn't really count when the plane is empty."

So we read the in-flight magazine and dreamed of what magic we would weave when we could be alone together in Barrow, Alaska.

Chapter 14

"That was...different," Eloise said. "Not what I expected from you, but still..."

"At least one woman has told me I have a strange mind," I said.

I was freezing as we laid nude side-by-side in a narrow double bed in the back room of the Nose Rub Hospitality House near the Barrow airport. We'd abandoned the plane when the temperature dropped precipitously. It'd been too cold in the frozen waste of December to stay the night on-board.

No trenchies. No yellow ochre. No sunrise either. Winter Solstice above the Arctic Circle. Soon we would be gone from here. Soon we would be heading up into the Brooks Range. But, not now. Not at this moment. Not at this time.

Eloise and I had cast the die. We'd sealed a deal that I don't think either one of us had expected to make in this or any incarnation. But, these were the musings of a fool. Things were mixed up now. We were mixed up now.

On her side, Eloise pressed her bare warm back against me. "I do like spooning."

"That's cool," I said. "I like forking."

She sighed. "What to do with you, Mitch."

"Well," I said. "I did like that thing you did when you were on top and—"

She rolled over and pressed a finger to my mouth. "That was just a warm-up."

A kiss. She tasted good. She had tasted good, too.

And, what had happened in the intervening hours when the two of us had been alone at last? Trip to the moon on gossamer wings? The best I'd ever had in any incarnation? The theme from *Love Story* playing over and over in the back of my mind? The theme of *Boogie Nights* playing over and over in my head?

A wise old sage of a man had once told me that a gentleman never reveals to others a lady's "indiscretions" that she'd hammered out on passion's anvil.

From this axiom, I'd extracted my own corollary: even if you're *not* a gentleman but want to get laid on a regular basis, you leave such things unsaid as well.

Aphrodite's spell on Eloise, such as it had been, had disappeared within ten minutes of being wheels down at the Barrow airport. That'd been okay, though. The spell of love had worked and was working its own magic on the two of us. I let myself fall into its warm pool. Let it take me down. Let everything go.

A man does not recover from such a devotion of the heart to such a woman! He ought not; he does not.

Perhaps that had been Aphrodite's gift after all. Not the obvious, but something much more subtle than even I could barely grasp. Perhaps yes. Perhaps no.

Not that I'm any kind of sentimentalist. Not me.

I was content now with just Eloise next to me in bed, her breathing quiet, her body warm and familiar next to mine.

This is what happens when you finally obtain the one. The one you've known for an eternity, which isn't forever; it's just a really long time. The one who you've always had in your heart even though you didn't know you had her in your heart.

There was no discussion of feelings or emotions. Why *would* there be? Why *should* there be? There are times, now and again, when a man and a woman unite with each other and there is no discussion of emotions, no "why won't you tell me what you're feeling," because she knows you so well that there's no need for such tripe.

There's no need for that kind of distraction.

Eloise and I had blended with each other. We'd finally acknowledged what each of us had wanted for so long. An end to loneliness. An end to that journey.

Be yourself, right? It's taken me so long to realize that would be how I would win her. The credo, *et cetera*. Who knew?

"We've slept almost nine hours," I said.

She sat upright with a start. "The calculations! Dammit, Mitch! You shouldn't have let me sleep this long."

Yeah, that spell was definitely gone. Definitely. Remember what I said about when two people and all that? Sometimes, it's the other things, too.

"We've got time," I said. "Wentworth told us she'd have us on the side of the mountain in three hours."

Eloise pushed the covers back and stood up. "That's the problem, Mitch. Which one? Which mountain? I still can't come up with a solution."

I should have been making eye contact with Eloise, but my eyes had better territory to cover. "Come back to bed."

Eloise put her hands on her ever so bare hips. "Our world as we know it is on the midst of collapse and that is all you can think about?"

"Yes."

She rolled her eyes and began dressing. "I can't channel the Void anymore. The Manifold is on the verge of collapse. I can't determine the exact flash point. Doesn't that bother you?"

"No," I pushed the covers back and heaved my legs over the side of the bed. My back was killing me. My cock was sore. I could still taste her on my lips. "We'll just go to Plan C."

"Plan C, right," Eloise said. "And do, pray tell, enlighten me as to what Plan C is."

"Simple. We get in Wentworth's helicopter and tell her to fly south for the Brooks Range," I said. I pulled on my heavy trousers. "Things will work out, Eloise. They always do."

"So, you're making it up as you go?"

"Something like that. I've always just gone with it. Gone with the flow, even when I can't feel the Flow. It's who I am," I rounded the bed and put my hands on her bare, muscular shoulders. "When the time comes, Eloise, you'll know what to do. Okay? Trust me."

"It's bad, Mitch," she said. "I can't nail it exactly. I've done the calculations ten times. Looks like we might truly be at the end of the road. The Manifold is barely holding. Why are you looking at me like that?"

"You're beautiful," I said.

Now, most women would swoon over a compliment like that.

Not her. Not Eloise.

"Please, Mitch. I'm having enough trouble with the flash point calculations without that—"

"I'm going to get some breakfast."

She smiled. "I could really use some tofu."

"Okay," I said.

Tofu. The lady wanted tofu, and I was going out into sub-zero temperatures to get it.

It must be love.

* * *

Total darkness at the top of the world. Forever night, here, the aurora roared silently overhead turning the white of the snow and tundra into a wavering green that always moved, always changed.

The cold was biting as I trudged through the snow-covered streets of Barrow. A certain quietude pressed down over the town, over the mood. Over my mood.

I'd picked up some breakfast. A couple of bentos from Osaka's. The woman liked tofu. What could I say? I'd taken the one with seal meat. I'd also downed a couple of sakes.

For the first time in several incarnations, I actually hoped z would pop in on me. No dice. He was nowhere. Perhaps he was in the plane, but perhaps he wasn't. It didn't really matter. In any event, I decided to see if I could drum him and Cooter up. I walked through the streets toward the Barrow airport, my boots making that heavy crunching sound with each step on the frozen snow.

I neared the fence line and saw the plane near the runway.

My token bag opened.

I dropped the bento boxes and made a grab for the bag, but my hand couldn't gain entry. Then, it closed again.

The roar of snowmobile engines caught my ear. I recovered the bentos and looked over the flat runway strip.

They were piling out of the back of the plane. The trenchies. Crawling all over the dull silver of the hull.

The crack! Dammit! That's how they'd been getting in. How could all of us have missed it?

Another Time Eddy swept by me. The bag promptly opened, yet I still couldn't get to the contents therein. The trenchie-driven snowmobiles were headed toward the airport gate. Before long, they'd be spilling out into the streets of Barrow looking for us.

Eloise! Dammit!

174

I ran through the night back to our room just in time to see Eloise take a trenchie down. I fieldstripped his corpse and re-covered a Glock pistol and a couple of clips and a bag of flares. Better than nothing.

"They're coming in through the plane," I said.

Eloise stiffened and picked up her duffle bag. "We need to leave. Now."

"Don't you want your tofu?" I asked, still holding the bentos.

Eloise shook her head.

We left through the bathroom window and ran through the snow-covered streets to the far edge of the Barrow airport. A lone black Bell 205 helicopter sat on the tarmac. The slim form of a woman in a heavy flight suit was peeling the heaters off the helicopter's engine mount.

"That's her?" Eloise said.

"Yes. Wentworth."

Eloise and I slowed and caught our breath. We didn't want to make it appear like we were being chased by that horde on the other side of the field that continued to pile out of the plane. Even though we were.

"Mr. Pimpkin," Captain Wentworth yelled. "You and your woman hurry up. We need to put some miles behind us if you want to be there on time."

"Sure," I said.

"And the money?" Wentworth said.

I tossed a bag of waded bills to her. Wentworth took a look then closed the bag. "That'll do. Get in."

Eloise bumped me. "Pimpkin?"

"Long story."

I looked toward the plane. More trenchies were there, but stood in mass without really moving. The Manifold must be dicking with them. They seemed to ignore us or not notice us. Not that it really mattered.

"Clear!" Captain Wentworth yelled.

A buzzing, then the helicopter's engine began winding up, the whoosh of the main blade above me in the light of the aurora.

"Come on, Mitch," Eloise said.

I threw in the bag containing the flares and the Glock, and I climbed in the back of the helicopter.

I was sliding the helicopter's heavy side door shut when something gave me pause.

Just out of sight on the edge of the tarmac he stood watching me. The aurora behind him, casting him in a red and green silhouette. It was him.

Marlow.

I slammed the door shut and gave Wentworth the thumbs up. Eloise and I put on the headphones letting the cables dangle on the floor.

"I still don't have the flash point!" she yelled. "What the fuck are we going to do? It opens in a little over three hours."

"Eloise," I said above the roar of the engine. "You can do this when the time comes. Be yourself. Be the brief. Forget the metaphysics and Aunt Jenny. Just feel your way there. I'll be with you."

"What's wrong?" she said.

I pointed toward the window.

She looked. "Shit."

As the helicopter went airborne and Wentworth banked it over the runway, I opened the window and stuck my hand out into the cold of the daynight that was this Winter Solstice.

I flipped off Marlow.

"That's so juvenile, Mitch. He can't even see it."

"It felt good, though," I said.

Through the rough static of the headphones, Captain Wentworth called back to me. "Pimpkin. Where the hell are we going?"

"Dead south. The Brooks Range."

* * *

"Holy Lolita," Wentworth whistled. "We're passing a caribou gathering site out there."

She pointed into the darkness of the Arctic. Nether Eloise nor I saw anything but the green aurora-lit tundra below us.

"We'll need to be careful," she said. "I once ran over a caribou in my car."

Captain Fredricka Wentworth. Our pilot. Wentworth was crazy all right.

They'd told me she was crazy last night when I'd sought her out at the Northern Lights Strip Club and Book Store in downtown Barrow. An old Eskimo had told me that Wentworth had always had a bit too much pride, and had a prejudice view of others based on her first impressions.

"Can she do it?" I'd asked.

"Best there is. Goes places no other pilot goes. Does that in the air, too. Holds her hand steady on the stick. Always. Never wavers."

Wentworth had just finished her all nude *Sense and Sensibility Review* to a sold out crowd in Barrow when I'd caught her attention.

"Yeah," Wentworth had said. "I can take you two. But it'll cost you. All cash."

That was more than fourteen hours ago. I looked at my watch in the dim of the helicopter's dashboard lights. It was two hours from the Winter Solstice. The bulk of the Brooks Range heaved up directly south of us.

I looked at Eloise. "Anything?"

"The Void is going!" Eloise said. "I can feel it slipping from me!"

"That doesn't sound good," I said.

"Are you two in love?" Wentworth said.

A pregnant beat. Neither Eloise nor I said anything.

"Ah, you must be," Wentworth said. "You're both speechless. Either that or the two of you had some really good sex recently—or both."

"How much longer till we're there, Captain?" Eloise asked.

"I was in love once," Wentworth started. "Asked him to marry me, but he turned me down. Bastard. Tell me not that I am too late, that such precious feelings from him are gone forever—we're at the foothills of the Brooks Range now."

Wentworth had this unsettling ability to turn completely around and talk to us, leaving the stick and instruments to themselves as she made some point about feelings, or emotional perfection. Times like these made me glad I had a cock to hold onto.

A white glaring flash burst above us.

"What the hell was that?" Wentworth said. "Shit! Engine's out! We're falling!"

Then, silence as the helicopter lost altitude. Wentworth grappled with the stick as I strapped into the back seat next to Eloise.

A jar.

The helicopter sat still, suspended in mid-air.

The whole of the midnight arctic tundra flashed with a burning white intensity, and I could make out every ravine, every canyon of the land below us. Then blackness and a roar that flew through us.

All silence. All is done.

The burn of the aurora hard overhead spreading out over the tundra; bright green landscape all around and the silence.

"The Manifold," Eloise muttered. "It's collapsed. It's over."

The helicopter hung stationary in mid air.

The aurora turned from green to a blood red.

Then, Wentworth began in a voice that sounded like the worst possible type of scratching on the blackboard.

"I've been summoned!" Wentworth said.

Only, it wasn't Wentworth. It was something else. It was someone else.

She removed her helmet and unbuckled herself and floated up in the cockpit before turning to face Eloise and me.

"What the hell is she going on about?" I said. "They told me she was crazy as hell. This takes the cake!"

"No, Mitch!" Eloise said. "It can't be happening now! We're almost there! She can't be here yet!"

"What are *you* talking about?" I said.

Eloise pointed to Wentworth. "The Time Witch!"

"I've been summoned!" the Time Witch repeated. "This Manifold is gone. All is at the single Union now. The single foci! Soon, the Gathering and the Dissolution. All will be at peace. Soon, all will be the Ultimate Death!"

"The Evil One?" I said to Eloise. "You can't be serious. That's all bullshit!"

"I've been summoned!" the Time Witch yelled. "The Manifold has collapsed! Marlow has summoned me. He's cast the die. Put things into motion. The Manifold has collapsed, Time Walkers! Time for you to die the Ultimate Death!"

"Fuck this!" I said.

I unstrapped and jumped out of my seat.

I shoved Wentworth against the wall. "Now, that is fantasy. Prime Movers are one thing. But, the Time Witch? The Destroyer of All Truth-Time? Give me a break. Could use some help here, Eloise!"

I struggled with Wentworth and kept her pinned against the bulkhead despite her repeated attempts to bite me. She was small but strong as hell. Eloise took some rope and tried to wrap it around Wentworth's hands, but she pushed both of us back against our seats.

"Time Walkers!" she said. "Your time is over! Your heresy will end! In two hours, all will be lost for your ilk. You have two hours!"

Eloise threw a first aid kit at her. "Shut up, you crazy bitch!"

"Just wait," Wentworth said. "You will see the signs before long."

Wentworth moved fast next to me and pointed at Eloise. "She will decide, that one. She'll decide between you and her. She'll decide to chose you!"

I shoved Wentworth away. She banged hard into the bulkhead. I pulled out the Glock.

"Wait, Mitch!" Eloise said.

I sighted the Time Bitch and plugged a clip into her, shooting out most of the helicopter's windshield in the process.

She lunged toward me, but not before Eloise pulled open the side door and, with a glancing blow, pushed her past us and out the helicopter's open door into the night air. Then, the Time Witch screamed as she plunged to the ground below us.

"Nice!" I said to Eloise.

"You can't kill her, Mitch," Eloise shouted. "Even if we could restore the Manifold, which is impossible, she'll be out there. Hunting you. Following you—"

We were both cut short by the sudden downward movement of the helicopter as whatever had been holding us in mid-air let go.

Eloise leaped past me and into the co-pilot's seat and took the stick.

The helicopter spun, and I was plastered against my seat as Eloise tried to bring the helicopter under control.

"Not good, Mitch!" Eloise yelled. "I can't fly this thing!"

"Then what in the hell are you doing in the pilot's seat?" I said.

She turned her head back to me. A moment, a look. "I'm making it up as I go."

The hump of the mountains loomed large out the windshield in front of us. "Shit!"

And, then, our pilotless helicopter began to auto rotate down to the broad white expanse of the snow-filled tundra north of the thrust up ridge of the Brooks Range.

Then, the drone of the altitude alarm.

For an instant, all was still. Time was immobile. The red aurora burned outside the helicopter's windows. The tall Range rose over us as we neared the ground. It was only a matter of time before—

And, the grind of shearing metal as the helicopter crashed down onto the tundra.

Eloise screamed.

Then, silence and the wind.

You pierce my soul. I'm half agony, half hope.

Chapter 15

The wreckage of the helicopter was strewn across the frozen tundra, as was the wreckage of Eloise. I don't know what anomaly of physics had left me unscathed. We had both been tossed from the copter on its death dive.

When I found her, she was still alive. Beaten, and battered, but alive. When I felt that first faint pulse, it was like a breath of spring had swept across the top of the world. I inspected the rest of her body, ignoring the impulse to indulge my memory of how I had inspected the rest of her body in bed only hours before.

Well, I tried to inspect her body, but the parka was thick and I wasn't about to remove it. She would need all the warmth she could get once shock set in. All I knew was she was unconscious, and something had to be broken if I could tell anything by the way she was lying.

The aurora borealis was the only source of light in that desolate wilderness. And it was ten-thirty in the morning.

My little horse must think it queer
To stop without a farmhouse near
Between the woods and frozen lake
The darkest morning of the year.

Only an hour-and-a-half until the end of the Time Walker infiniteverse—according to those who are supposedly in the know.

I had no sense of direction until I made out the form of the mountains in the middle distance. Much too far to walk in such a short time.

I caressed Eloise's face. She was unconscious. I prayed to the supreme being of all infiniteverses to have pity on the woman I had come to love.

She opened her eyes.

Damn, it's much easier to ignore the supreme being when it ignores your requests for miracles.

She moaned. I stroked her cheek.

"Mitch," she said.

I shushed her and kissed her.

She moved her arm tentatively, and then she raised her hand and touched my face.

"Are you okay?" she asked.

"Never mind me. How are you? Where does it hurt?"

"It doesn't hurt."

"That's good," I said.

"No, that's bad," she said. "I told you I would die getting you to your flash point."

"Well then, you're not going to die yet because we aren't at my flash point."

"I can only move my arm, Mitch."

"Can you get into my token bag?"

Eloise was silent for a while. I wasn't sure if she had lost consciousness again or was trying to access the bag.

"No, I can't," Eloise said, "The Manifold is annihilated."

"We still have ninety minutes, give or take. We'll find a way."

Then a sound like the tinkling of a bell echoed in the distance. First so faintly I could not tell if I was imagining it.

Then as it drew nearer, I became more confident in its existence. A lantern glowed. It was a dog sled, and driving the dog sled was the maddest man I had ever known, singing "Monotonously Rings the Bell"—in Russian no less.

"z!" I shouted. Then I joined him in singing the last verse.

Однозвучно гремит колокольчик,
И дорога пылится слегка.
И замолк мой ямщик, а дорога
Предо мной далека, далека...

"Mitch," Eloise said. "You're a horrible singer."

"Nice to see you haven't lost your sense of humor, my love."

z pulled the dog sled up next to us.

"Good to see you, z."

"No time for that, Mitch," z said in as serious a voice I had ever heard from him. "Come with me."

"But Eloise."

At that, Cooter jumped from under a caribou hide in the dog sled.

"Cooter will take care of everything, Mitch."

"Cooter? How will Cooter take care of anything?"

"Damn it, Mitch. I'm a doctor," Cooter said. And he proceeded to treat Eloise.

z led me off behind a snowdrift.

"What is it, z?"

"No time for blame, Mitch, but this is what happens when you fail to follow my instructions. I told you the Palouse Range, and I meant the fucking Palouse Range."

"Fuck you, z," was all I could think to say.

His face was drawn. I had never seen him so haggard.

"The Manifold has fallen, Mitch."

"So I've gathered."

"And time is short if we're going to do anything about it."

"And you're talking."

"It's a courtesy, porridge head. I'm here to let you know the choice is on you."

"What choice?"

"Eloise can give you a mini-flash to your flash point."

"So what's the problem with that?"

"It will kill her."

"No way, z."

"Then you choose the total and complete and final destruction of the Time Walker infiniteverse."

"Fuck you, z," was again all I could think to say.

"We'll all become trenchies," z said. "Sycophants of Dr. Hodge."

"But alive," I clarified.

z sighed. "If you call that being alive."

"That's a hell of a choice, Hobson."

"Fuck you, Mitch. I told you never to call me by my last name."

z led me back to Cooter and Eloise. I had never seen z without his persistent veneer of gaiety. Maybe Cooter wasn't putting out.

Eloise looked at me with a meaningfulness I hadn't seen since Idaho.

"I see you haven't lost your venal sense of humor," Eloise said. She was standing next to Cooter—leaning on him, but standing no less. I was afraid of her again.

"So you can read my mind again, can you?" I said. Eloise looked at Cooter and smiled.

z shook his head and waved his hand abruptly at Cooter. "No games Coot, you've healed her too well."

Cooter touched Eloise on the nose.

"And I always thought our Time Walker witch doctors were crackpots," I thought to myself as privately as possible.

Eloise just stared at me.

"We are crackpots, Mitch, but she won't be reading your mind," Cooter said.

"We can't have her ability to read your mind interfere with your choice when the time comes," z said.

"What if I don't make a choice?" I said.

z shook his head. "Not making a choice is itself a choice."

The sound of a high-pitched whine filled the air. Then another and another. A chorus of disharmonious snowmobile engines grew louder.

So that's what those snowmobiles on the plane were for!

"Trenchies," Cooter said.

"Into the dog sled," z said.

Cooter, Eloise, and I jumped into the dog sled, and z cracked the whip. Off we went into the aurora's psychedelic darkness.

Soon, the trenchies on snowmobiles appeared as black dots on the edge of the visible world. Cooter pulled a .50 caliber machine gun from under a blanket and blasted away.

The dog sled moved along at a rate I had never known possible. These had to be alpha dogs from the Time Walker special forces K-10 unit.

One snowmobile exploded in a ball of flame. Cooter wasn't too bad a shot on the move.

Eloise clinged to me. I embraced her. I had never known her to be so frightened.

"We must get close enough, Mitch."

"Close enough for what?"

"Close enough for me to be able to mini-flash you to your flash point."

Two snowmobiles crossed in front of us, determined to slow us down, but Cooter picked the trenchies off cleanly. They fell away and the snowmobiles continued riderless, and for all I know are still grazing the land to the north. The land of snow and ice.

"I'm not going to do it, Eloise."

"Do what, Mitch?"

"I'm not sacrificing you."

Eloise went cold. Her eyes had a ferocity I had never known from a woman before. It was even more ferocious than the look I've seen after losing control and finishing inside a woman without protection.

"Mitch, it is my brief to die. You will get to that flash point. That is your brief."

"I love you, Eloise. I won't let you die."

Three more snowmobiles pursued us across a frozen river. Cooter dropped a grenade over the ice. It exploded under the last of the snowmobiles. *Only two to go.*

I looked at z.

z simply mushed on while Cooter emptied a clip at his quarry.

"It's no time to be selfish, Mitch," Eloise said.

"Selfish? I'm thinking entirely of you."

"And what about all the other Time Walkers in the infiniteverse?"

"Didn't I tell you last night you are the only Time Walker in my infiniteverse?" Mitch said.

"Fucking pillow talk, this is real life!"

z stopped the dog sled. The two snowmobiles zipped past us, one of them flying over the edge of a cliff. Five seconds passed before we heard the explosion. The other snowmobile teetered on the edge. The trenchie jumped off and let his machine fall over the edge.

Cooter went after the trenchie. They embraced in mortal hand-to-hand combat.

"This ain't no game, Mitch," z said. "We're depending on you."

"Why me?"

"It's never a question of why. Only 'what next.'"

"So what next?"

Cooter and the trenchie fell from view, having pulled each other over the cliff.

"Cooter!" z shouted, but for some reason, he had a gleam in his eye. "Out of the sled, you two. This is as far as I take you."

Eloise and I obeyed.

"What now, z?"

"I'm off to check on Cooter. You see, Mitch. You're not the only one being asked to sacrifice for the good of the infinite-verse."

z steered the dogs away from the cliff.

"I mean what now for us?" I said.

"Be yourself," z said, and off he went, but before he was out of earshot, he called out over his shoulder, "And remember what your mother always said: never eat yellow ochre snow," he was gone.

And indeed, the snow all around us was turning yellow ochre.

* * *

Why had he mentioned my mother? Yes, he meant it rhetorically, but he knows how much I long to know about my childhood, my life before my first incarnation. Where did I come from? I don't know any Time Walkers who know where they came from, but none of them seem bothered by it.

I want to know.

And yet it seems to be a fool's errand to pursue such knowledge.

Now our world is falling apart, although I still have my doubts, but the intensity of this episode puts me in a primal state of mind. Where did I come from, and why did I end up here? And why must it end now? Why here? And in the end, must it really end here after all? And was I willing to take that chance?

* * *

"Mitch, I need the device before I flash you," Eloise said.

"It's in my token bag," I said.

"So give it to me, hodgedamnit!"

And sure enough, as I put my hand at my side, the token bag appeared, and I had access to its entire contents.

z?

I handed Eloise the device.

A dog barked in the distance. I wondered why z was returning.

"I'm sorry Mitch, I'm still having trouble with the calculations."

"Forget it, I'm not going. Just use the device and we'll see what happens."

Eloise looked at me like I was a total idiot.

"I can't while you are here. It would all be over. You are our last hope, Mitch. You must get to that flash point. Only twenty minutes left."

"I will take you with me."

"I will die either way."

"Mini-flash with me. I'll find a way to save you."

"How? You don't even know what's going on."

"I'll just be myself. I will protect you. Get us to the flash point and you will see."

Eloise began to weep.

"Why are you crying? I didn't mean it to sound so melodramatic."

"I'm crying because I can't calculate the coordinates to the flash point, Mitch."

"What do you mean? You're the expert on Sardonics. Best score in class, right?"

"Second best," she confessed.

"Well, other than John."

"And the truth is, I only scored so well because I slept with Rufus T."

"Come on, Eloise. Everyone knows that. Can we cut out the confessions and get to work? You're an experienced Time Walker. You can do it."

"But I don't know how. I can't figure it out. The rules don't work anymore."

"Fuck the rules, El! You can do it. Just be yourself. Or do you just want to go find a log cabin with me and fuck me while we wait for the end of the world?"

"We must save our infiniteverse, but I can't do it, Mitch. I want to so badly, but I just can't deliver." Her weeping turned into hysteria. "I'm a fraud!"

In another world, in another time, I would have slapped her. But Time Walkers have become too sophisticated for that. They haven't become too sophisticated to change behaviors that beg for a slapping, but so be it. I had to dig deeper for another solution.

I created a Time Closet. Fifteen minutes would still leave five minutes to enter the flash point, assuming all went well.

It was the first time I had created a Time Closet with another person. Eloise embraced me.

We had a quickie.

It's what I had always wanted to do in my Time Closet. And when the end of the world is at hand, you can't imagine how intense the erotic impulse is.

Eloise looked at me. "I'm sorry, Mitch."

"Eloise. I don't believe you are going to die. But I do believe you can get us to the flash point. I need you to relax and feel the coordinates. You are the one always talking about feelings, right? And yet you get so caught up in superficial feelings that you forget how deep your feelings actually go. You have the answers within. Just feel it."

"I'm afraid, Mitch."

"I'm losing the Time Closet; it's go time."

"No, Mitch. Not so fast!"

And yet, there we were, so soon. Oh, too soon out of the Time Closet and on the snowy, freezing precipice of the cliff in the heart of the Brooks Range.

Eloise had composed herself.

"Once I flash you, Mitch, you'll have five minutes to enter the flash point. I'll have to detonate the device. You can't be on this side of the flash point when I do, or all is lost."

"I'm taking you with me."

"I'm flashing you, Mitch, and I'm staying behind, and there's nothing you can do about it."

She closed her eyes, but I grabbed her just before I was blinded by the strobe of white light that filled the visible world.

The mini-flash.

And on the other side of the flash, I was on a mountainside and the rainbow glow of the flash point was only thirty yards up the slope. Eloise was in my arms. She was as surprised as I had ever seen her.

"I told you that you wouldn't die," I said. "I knew you had it in you to pull us both through."

"She pulled us through too," the voice said from nearby.

A dog approached us, limping.

Marlow. On cross-country skis. Towing a long black box behind him on runners. The casket.

"Now you will both die, and I will bring about the Omniverse," Marlow said. He pulled out a Glock he had tucked in his pants in the small of his back. "Thank you for the device."

"I'll detonate it!" Eloise said.

"Not with Mitch here you won't. Then your infiniteverse and all infiniteverses and the Omniverse will all be annihilated. You don't want that on your conscience, do you?"

Marlow stood between the flash point and me.

Two minutes remaining.

"Maybe I won't have to kill you," Marlow said. "Maybe you could just play nice and give me the device, and I'll drop it in the flash point. You're infiniteverse will be gone, but you can join me as agents of the Omniverse."

"Mitch, don't listen to him," Eloise said. She said it as much to steel herself as to hearten me. "Get to the flash point so I can blow this fucker."

A swarm of trenchies were making their way up the mountain. A flood of them.

"Join us, Mitch. Join us, Eloise."

"We'll live for freedom, Dr. Hodge!" Eloise screamed, letting the cat out of the bag regarding Marlow's identity. "Freedom! Let all infiniteverses exist with their own unique characteristics, and to hell with the oppression of the Omniverse!"

One minute remaining.

Marlow fired the Glock directly between Eloise's eyes.

"Marlow!" I yelled.

But the slug stopped, suspended in mid-air between the muzzle of the Glock and the vital soft tissue of my lover's head.

John had materialized from out of nowhere with the slug pinched between his fingers.

"Where'd you come from, John?" Marlow said, and he unloaded the entire clip from the handgun into John's body, but the slugs passed through without any apparent effect. When the gun was empty, Marlow and his dog attacked John, but John subdued them.

"Mitch," John said, "get the fuck into the flash point now. You have thirty seconds."

"Not without Eloise," I said.

Marlow's dog ran off to lick its wounds. Marlow tried to get the device from Eloise, but John crushed his skull with a heavy rock. The rising tide of trenchies steadily approached.

"You understand I am to be sacrificed now too," John said.

"What do you mean?" I asked.

"Because you are dragging your feet. They sent me with the message. Now I'm here to be annihilated along with Eloise and the trenchies when Eloise detonates the device. I'll be annihilated, thanks to you."

"I love you, John. I love you, Eloise. Why do they send the ones I love to be sacrificed? It's like they are using you as hostages."

"It was written from the beginning that Eloise would die. Had you accepted it and done your duty, my death would not have been necessary. Now I die because of you."

"Then I will die too and to hell with everything else. Detonate the device, Eloise."

"What about your mother?" John asked.

I was stunned. "My mom?"

"They will send her as the final resort, and then she will die too and her death also will be on your head. Or you can get your ass into the flash point where she waits for you. You'll save her and the rest of the Time Walkers."

I looked at Eloise.

"Go, Mitch," she said.

"Come with me, John," I said.

"Only room for one," he said, and raised his hand, pointing to the flash point. "You only have five seconds. Go!"

I turned and ran up the mountain slope toward the flash point without one last long lingering look behind.

Three seconds, two…

"I love you," Eloise and John called out in unison as I lunged into the flash point.

As the seal closed around me, I turned and saw the tren-chies envelop John and Eloise, and then Eloise touched the device.

Eloise, John, and the trenchies disappeared.

Everything went dark.

Chapter 16

Truth is feeling. Feeling is truth.

A girl I once knew had told me that long ago in a different Truth-Time, in a different incarnation. But the same. At the time, I hadn't believed her any more than I believed anyone in any of my incarnations. But, none of that matters anymore.

Light.

Then cold. And snow.

Shit! It didn't work!

I opened my eyes, the jump completed. It was late afternoon. A sun hung low in the sky over the round hills of the mountains around me.

What is truth? What is time? How the two intermingled to forge my reality, my existence, my brief, is still a mystery to me.

As I said before, I'm not Tech.

I stood on another mountain now. Not in Alaska, not in the Brooks Range. My flash point cut hard over the ridge as it dissolved behind me in a fury of noise and heat. It'd come. I'd come. It'd been good.

I sat on a nearby log.

The air was warmer here, not the biting cold of above the Arctic Circle. I stripped off the heavy jacket I'd put on a mere five hours ago in Barrow.

The flash point collapsed fully with thunderous applause, then all was quiet, all was still. The burn of hot ozone blew past me.

I hadn't made an Assumption.

I was dressed as I had been just moments ago on the Brooks Range.

With John.

With Eloise.

"I've seen the permutations," she'd told me not so long ago. "I die in one hundred percent of the scenarios."

I opened my token bag and pulled it out. The astrolabe. Our astrolabe.

Eloise. Eloise.

I fingered it in my hand, turned it over and over. Something wasn't right. This wasn't a typical jump. I'd jumped somewhere, but...

Loose gravel crunched behind me.

Mom?

No, z was simply getting sloppy in this incarnation.

"What in the hell do you want?" I said, keeping my back to him.

z started. "You know, Mitch—"

"I've lost it all. Lost her," I shoved the astrolabe back in my token bag.

z continued, "There is a strength in love that crosses both truth and time. You can't break it. You can't fight it."

"Save it, z," I said. "Where's my mother?"

"Your mother?"

"They lied to get me into the flash point, didn't they?"

"Expedience is the mother of deception, laddy," z said. "Or is that the mother of invention? Or the soul of brevity?"

Bastards.

"Forget it," I said, "Where am I this time?"

z pointed to the sign on the other side of a well-worn trail: "Hiawatha Bike Trail."

"We're at your first flash point, my boy," z said. "Just where I said you needed to be all along. You're actually listening to me this brief. Too bad it's ending all too soon. I'm rather enjoying it."

"What?" I said. "I don't get this at all."

He stood behind me as we both looked into the West. "In the Palouse Range. The Winter Solstice is in ten minutes. You've almost completed your brief, Mitch. Truth-time has smoothed out its pesky little wrinkles."

"If it's the Solstice, then she..."

I stood up. A surge of emotion flowed through me, weakening me at the knees. It heaved through me.

z moved next to me. "Be yourself, Mitch. It's really that simple. The Manifold has been restored. I know, I know. I take all the credit for it. I was the one who pushed you to complete your brief, my boy. I'll put in a good word for you with Aunt Jenny. Might even get you a bonus, or a promotion—but don't count on it! Ah, here she comes."

Below us some five hundred feet, my truck was flying up an old Forest Service road with three cop cars giving chase, sirens and lights ablaze.

Eloise!

As she was. As she had been. As the brief was. As the brief had been.

Eloise—in my pickup truck burning up the hill in the red burn of the late-afternoon Winter Solstice day.

z moved off. "Mind the time, Mitch. You have one more thing to do, lest you forget. One last item on your 'to do' list. You've got less than ten minutes. Don't miss your jump. I'm counting on you. We all are. *Adieu.*"

Eloise floored my rig up the skinny road toward me. The three cop cars closed on her, then suddenly I heard the Time

Crack as my first and final flash point blossomed less than a hundred feet away.

Eloise brought the pickup to a grinding halt next to me.

The flash point's frontal boundary blew past me. Blew past Eloise. Each of the trenchie-driven police cars dissolved in unison as the wave pushed down and out through the valley. A cloud of yellow ochre dust was all that remained and was picked up on the cold winter wind blowing through the Valley.

"Mitch!" Eloise yelled. "You made it! What took you so long!?"

We found each other. She took my hands.

I thought a thought and smiled.

She stared at me blankly. "What?"

I put a finger up to my head. "Are you getting this?"

"The Manifold has been restored," she said. "A new Void is there. I can't read your thoughts anymore. You must have made your flash point. I'm glad you're here."

I was stunned. "Don't you remember, Eloise? Our night in Barrow? The Brooks Range?"

She looked surprised and pointed to the undulating flash point in front of us. "What the hell are you talking about, Mitch? You must mean my duplicate. She was annihilated when you made your flash point in the Brooks Range."

"So you know?" I asked her. I needed to know how much she knew or remembered about my experiences with her duplicate.

"I know enough, Mitch," she said. "All that matters now is that you have to make your jump!"

Finally, the sun was setting. The sky red. The flash point had fully formed and waited for me, its throbbing slit open. Welcoming. The warmth of it.

I took Eloise in my arms.

"Why are you trying to hug me? Why are you—"

"I love you, Eloise," I said. "I always have."

"You love me? When did this happen?"

I kissed her. Hard.

She broke from me. "This is a surprise. Especially from you, Mitch."

"You're alright with this?"

She smiled. "Yeah. Night in Barrow, eh? You have me at a disadvantage."

"Don't worry. Although, there is this one thing you do with your..."

She shoved me toward the flash point. "Go. Don't worry. I'll see you on the Otherside. 'All the world's a stage,' isn't that what they say?"

"Something like that."

I left her and walked up the slope feeling the flash point's warmth as I neared. I turned back to her one last time.

And, then I entered the flash point. It closed around me.

Then brightness.

I jumped.

* * *

Always the Sardonics.

Darkness. The smell of burning wood. The smell of humans. The smell of theater.

"Come on! Come on!" a voice came from beside me. "It's your scene! Go!"

z droned on and on. "London in 1600. You can't get a good meal anywhere. Although the Tower of London serves a decent bit of nosh."

From the stage beside the pit, I stared up from the open amphitheater to the tapestry of stars above London. It's a nice break from the routine, this new incarnation. This new brief.

The Apothecary moved across the stage and handed me the vial:

Put this in any liquid thing you will
And drink it off, and if you had the strength
Of twenty men, it would dispatch you straight.

I took the vial and turned back to the crowd:

There is thy gold- worse poison to men's souls,
Doing more murther in this loathsome world,
Than these poor compounds that thou mayst not sell.

The Earl was near the props watching his players performing his play the best they could. It was even a challenge for me. Not Juliet, though.

Through the smoke and noise from the pit, I saw her just off stage waiting to come on. She smiled and gave me a wink.

How they had said she'd pass for a boy and be on stage, I'd yet to figure out. But, Aunt Jenny did have connections here and there. Not so much bending the rules, but bending the Truth-Time. Who was I to judge? I'd rather kiss her than that French understudy Philip. But, z always said I never recognized talent.

Thou desperate pilot, now at once run on
The dashing rocks thy seasick weary bark!
Here's to my love! [Drinks.] O true apothecary!
Thy drugs are quick. Thus with a kiss I die.

And with that, I fell back onto the stage, landing so I could keep watch backstage while appearing dead front stage. Yeah, I know theater.

Juliet was on stage with z. Why the Earl cast him as the Friar, who knew? But there you are.

What's here? A cup, clos'd in my true love's hand?
Poison, I see, hath been his timeless end.
O churl! drunk all, and left no friendly drop
To help me after? I will kiss thy lips.
Haply some poison yet doth hang on them
To make me die with a restorative.

Juliet kneeled and put her lips to mine. I pressed my tongue. She hit me.

Thy lips are warm!

And Marlow?
I'd seen him in the crowd before the play had started. He wasn't really a fan, though. He's moved on to blank verse or Dido or whatever. He'd added an "e" to his last name to try to get some mileage. I, however, never had liked his writing. Or, his dog.
The end of the play was drawing near. I had it easy. Just lie there on stage and wait for the final words. Whatever they were. We'd only read the damn thing that morning.
Juliet rose and stood next to me. The warmth of her. The smell of her. So close.
She turned to z who stood nearby in his cloak.

Go, get thee hence, for I will not away.

z didn't move.
Out of the corner of my eye, the Earl looked at his script, and then looked back at z. He pointed to exit, stage right. z ignored him.
Juliet paused, and then cleared her throat and ad libbed.

Perhaps you didn't hear me, my good friar.

Go, get thee hence, for I will not away.

The crowd grew silent.

"No, madam, no!" z yelled in character. "I will not depart yon virgin woman in thoust hour of need! Yea, no!"

Philip, in his slick nasal French accent, pushed out the watch's lines:

Lead, boy. Which way?

z yelled. "Stay out!"
Juliet started:

Yea, noise? Then I'll be brief. O happy dagger!
This is thy sheath...

"No!" z said. "Fare, Juliet! Your Romeo doth lives!"
z kicked me in the ribs hard.
"Shit!" I said. I rolled over and grabbed my side.
Shouts of glee erupted from the pit. "Yes!"
z pulled me up on my feet. "Rise yon Romeo! Rise!"
Philip attempted to come on stage with his lines:

the ground is, er, not bloody. Search about the
  churchyard.

"No, no!" z said. He threw a chair at Philip. "Out ye Haverland dog! Out! This couple must copulate with compunction! Anon, anon."

z looked at Juliet. "Is this a dagger I see before me?"
He snatched the dagger from her hand.
The Earl of Cambridge shook his head and threw the script on the floor. Marlow'e' was no doubt pleased.

z turned to the pit in very dramatic fashion. He walked to the center of the stage to face the crowd.

He placed the dagger above him with the point of the blade on his chest.

"With this dagger, I must commit," z said and plunged the blade in. Acting, of course.

The crowd gasped, punctuated by a few "oh, no's."

z sat down on the floor, still holding the dagger.

He motioned to Juliet and me. "Go way, Romeo and Juliet! Fare thee well and get off my stage. For the play's the thing, you know, to find out if you can get more bling."

Juliet took my hand and pulled me offstage.

z stared at the crowd.

> *Now is the time to be or not to be.*
> *MacBeth and Lear! You and Ophelia*
> *Must lie a threesome pair in a chastley*
> *Nunnery! And let not spells or potions*
> *Most fowl be a rooster herald of dawn.*
> *Yea! The cock doth ticketh o'well!*
> *For thy dawn tolling of fowl and men lay*
> *His gay comparisons apart, and answer me*
> *Manwise, sword against sword, ourselves alone!*
> *Fighting like cocks till the very last bone!*
> *Lo! On a Cootation plain I wait for*
> *Thee. While hither, her body, is next to*
> *Him. To the undiscovered country*
> *I blow thee down! Betwixt is my codpiece!*

Amidst the sound of women's and men's crying from the audience, z slipped down onto his side.

The Earl moved next to me. "They like it! This might be just the thing to catch the crowd's purse and..."

He looked up to the nubile young women in the balcony.

"...some finer things, too."

Out! Out! Damn Horatio spots from my mouth!
Behold I have a weapon upon a
Soldier's thigh: I have seen the day good man!
Alas, no honesty here! Then is
The Doomsday Manifold near and to
Each of us a little light must shine bright,
Before sad knife, I must decline. Really!
Adieu, ado, ado! And on the French
I poo poo! To hell with my life and the
blade I run! But have no pity for me!
To Mitch the Bitch I fare thee well! Over
Hill or dale the cock ticking prevails!
Something always comes of nothing! So shut
Your pyehole before my vengence does! You've
Been o'askin' for it for so long now!
Clamp thy mouth before I slap it tight shut!
The Bitch is on the fuckin' prowl o'er
The night! Before the evensong is sung
Time shall unfold what plaited raw and nice
Cunninglingus brings with pleasantries! O
Be gone poor world, I've had enough!
Even though the cock is ticking, thou will
Not knowest since yon codpiece is sticking!

z fell back and rolled over and died as the rain began pouring into the Globe.

A glooming peace this morning with it brings.
The sun for sorrow will not show his head.
Go hence, to have more talk of these sad things;
Some shall be pardon'd, and some punished;

Filling the Void

For never was a story of more woe
Than of this Friar and his lover, Joe.

"Now that's tragedy!" The Earl shouted as he furiously scratched the words down. "I love this ending! I've got to re-write it. I did like the bit about the codpiece, though. I might use that."

z jumped up and bowed. The crowd roared.

z looked back at us and smiled. "Don't worry, Earl. I'll stop by tonight and we can act it out together. I'll be Juliet, of course."

Juliet moved next to me. "Different ending than I remember. But, that's z."

z pulled me aside. "All's well that ends, Mitch. I told you not to worry. Now, have you ever been to Paris in the summer of 1938? No? Don't worry. You'll be there in a flash."

I threw Juliet a look. "I'd love to see you can-can."

She rolled her eyes as only she can-can. "I bet you would, Mitch. I bet you would."

"My audience awaits," z said.

He ran and threw himself mosh-like off the stage and into the crowded pit. I watched as they carried him off, flat on his back, with Cooter sitting on his chest.

And, what of John?

He's made his own path. At least that's the scuttlebutt I've heard back at HQ. He's beyond this Omniverse. He's crossed the Void. Never to return. Well, in theory anyway. Like I've said, that's the problem with the Sardonics. They're not perfect. And, I'm not Tech.

Alas, though, I've found that the Omniverse is really not that complicated. All you really need is the love of a good woman and a credo to live by. The rest of it just happens.

Be yourself.

I gave Juliet a wink.

"Her ladyship, Queen Elizabeth."

I bowed low as Aunt Jenny came to Juliet and me and the other players. "Your majesty."

Even I must admit she looked pretty hot in that ruff and hat. For an old bitch, that is.

I dropped to one knee in front of her.

Aunt Jenny fanned herself and motioned me to her side.

"You still really fucked this one, Mitch," she whispered low and slow.

I rolled my eyes.

She grabbed my ear and twisted it. Juliet snickered.

"John's run amok!" she wheezed. "And you're the only one I can spare to send after him." She shoved at my head and released my burning ear. "Meet z after the production party. He'll give you your brief."

Like I said, nothing is perfect.

Now. Anyone know where I can get a decent drink around here?

Feedback

P.D. Kew would love to hear what you think about this book. Send feedback to:

pd.kew.writer@gmail.com

www.ingramcontent.com/pod-product-compliance
Lightning Source LLC
Chambersburg PA
CBHW032003240626
47153CB00003B/1096